Prayer Agents
"Impacting the World for the Kingdom of God"

by
Jackie A. Jones Jr.

Prayer Agents by Jackie A. Jones Jr.

Copyright

Publishing company:
KDP publishing. Self-published by Jackie Jones Jr

For more information please visit:
www.jackiejonesjr.com

Graphic designer:
Justin Dortch
J. Dortch Graphic Design & Printing, LLC
Jdortchgraphics@gmail.com

Editor:
Alysha Sharpe

Illustrations:
www.thoughtco.com
www.google.com
www.encyclopediaofchicago.com
www.wikipedia.com

Unless otherwise indicated, all scriptural references are taken from the King James, Amplified, Message Bible, New Living Translation, New International Version of the Holy Bible

ISBN-978-0-578-67901-3

Dedications:
This book is dedicated to

My mom, Prophetess Beverly Jones, who kept me in prayer service as a child and taught me the true meaning of "fighting a good warfare" in prayer. My Father, Elder Jackie Jones Sr, who has been my rock during rough times of my life.

My spiritual parents, Archbishop William Hudson III and Pastor Andria Hudson who has instilled spiritual wisdom, pulled on the anointing that is on my life, and allowed me to flow freely in my spiritual gifts. I am a greater vessel to be used by God because of your leadership.

My daughter, Tiara "my guardian angel." who loves her daddy so much and constantly makes him proud every day.

Alexia Huggins, you prophesied to me years ago when you gave me a notebook that had the words "WRITE" on the cover and said I will one day write a book. Thank you for the push, the encouragement, the support and the impact you made on me while writing this book.

The Powerhouse Chicago, my church family who has been a staple in my life.

My spiritual mentor, Regina Crider "my favorite", who pulled the depth of intercession out of me. It is definitely because of you that I have learned the true meaning of coming boldly before the throne of grace.

My Support System: Qiana Jones (my sister), Kenneth Johnson Jr, Alysha Sharpe, LaTisha Morris, Kenyetta Shepard, Shaundrece Dixon, and Tracy Williamson, thank you for the push, inspiration, and encouragement to make this book come to pass.

Prayer Agents, to all praying people out here still believing, still interceding, still seeking the kingdom of God. We are helpers one to another. Let us continue to go after the heart of God and release in the earth the voice, the will, and the thoughts that lies in the mind of God.

Table of Contents

<u>Words from the Author</u>

"WHAT I DO BY FAITH, FAVOR WILL BACK ME UP"

You may ask Jackie, why this book? What separates this book on prayer from any other book? How am I guaranteed to know that my prayer will work?

I can assure you there will be times where you will see the hand of God move upon your prayers. There will also be times of silence where it seems as if God is no longer speaking or moving on your behalf. Let us be real for a moment. There are times where you pray, fast, confess the word and it seems like you are running into a brick wall. When you reach moments like that, that is the time where you need information and inspiration to continue a life of prayer. The more you continue praying beyond what you are experiencing in life, know that it is all contributing to the great manifested promise God is going to release in your life.

March 20, 2019, I was in prayer early that morning. The Lord led me to pray live on my social media platforms. I was led to do so on Facebook as well as Instagram. I will never forget the nervous feeling I had within me. I was not used to praying publicly via social media. The Lord led me to share with the people some scriptures regarding the power of prayer, and then I began to pray. I remember how the spirit of God took over the prayer and I felt as if it was just Him and I in an intimate space. After the live ended, I remember just praising God aloud, as I felt like His mission to ignite the people to pray was accomplished. The next two months the Lord charged me to pray every

Thursday at 9am via Facebook live and Instagram live. Every week the numbers of viewers increased and so did the testimonies. I would receive text messages and emails on how people were not just blessed but how they were ignited to pray. The Prophetic would flow through me as I would pray and minister to the people of God.

After three months of consistent prayer, I was faced with personal turmoil that I was not prepared for. The challenge came where I had to shift my life relationally and make adjustments that centered around me. It was a season of the unexpected leaving me to feel hopeless, doubtful, and even hurt but the Lord was consistent in my life. I'd experienced a season where I literally felt as if I could not pray and God would not hear me if I did.

What I did not realize was during the three months of consistent prayer, I was being covered and prepared for what was soon to come. The next several months, I spent time rebuilding, refocusing, and centering myself with the Lord in prayer and consecration. How did I do that you ask? It took for me to get tired of living life without God, tired of living out of anger, resentment and regret. Yes, we are human, and we experience very turbulent times in our lives. However, it does not mean because you go through persecution, pain, and disappointment that you have left God or that He has left you. In some cases, we have taken breaks or disconnect ourselves in a sense to reflect on where we are. God being so gracious to us, He will wait on us to come back to Him. THANK YOU, LORD! God knows that one day you will get tired of doing life on your own and will come back to Him for restoration.

April 7, 2020, while in my private prayer time with the Lord, He pressed upon my spirit to pray for senior leaders of churches all over the world. As I was concluding my prayer, the spirit of the Lord told me to go live on Facebook and pray. I was so hesitant as I have not gone live in almost one year. I followed the Lord and it was amazing the response I received from Pastors, Bishops, and Ministers who tuned in.

One week later, April 15th and April 16th, The Lord gave me a word for the people of God that he was sending mass economic relief and debts would be canceled. He gave me this word in prayer and told me to go live AGAIN.

By this time, I said ok, Lord maybe this is going back to our normal schedule. Testimonies were pouring in like crazy on how those who watched the live service was receiving unexpected checks and cash. It was mind blowing.

There was one prayer that occurred one Thursday where the Lord led me to pray for parents. The prayer was for parents to be truthful with themselves on what they have dealt with in their lives. God really ministered through me for parents to be healed from rejection, molestation, abandonment, and for them to be transparent with their children so they can also be healed.

The same day as well as days after, testimonies were shared from a great number of people on how they were healed from suicide, depression and even family secrets of past rapes and molestation. HALLELUJAH!

What is the purpose of my sharing this information? Simply this, when you doubt yourself, when you go through tough times that shifts your life, when you do not understand what is coming…DON'T STOP PRAYING! God wants to use you in a way you cannot even imagine. If I was not obedient to God when He told me to go live on social media or took those months to be restored in his presence. The testimonies would not have come, and those people may not have been healed, delivered and set free from the bondage they are in.

God gave me this in prayer:

"What I do by FAITH, FAVOR will back me up"

Prayer Agents by Jackie A. Jones Jr.

<u>Purpose of This Book</u>

I want to devote this book to new believers in Christ who are unknowledgeable on how to begin, ignite and engage in prayer. In addition to new believers, I am also targeting those individuals who have been groomed in prayer over the years on how to advance, mature, and develop a new passion for prayer. Utilizing the word of God as a guide, it is my desire to provide these targeted audiences with some essential tools, spiritual insight, and encouragement on how to pursue a lifestyle of effective prayer. Ultimately, the goal is for every person who reads this book to be charged, challenged and commissioned to become prayer vessels, conduits, and open portals yielded to God for the service of His kingdom.

The writing of this book is based upon my life. Through various challenging circumstances I sought an avenue in the realm of the spirit guaranteed to ignite, educate, and inspire the prayer agent inside of every believer who is willing to do the work. Prayer and Intercession are two supernatural divine tools used to combat the enemy, interrupt plots, plans and schemes sent out by demonic forces, and connects us to the power and voice of God.

The inspiration behind the writing of this book stems from a few pivotal moments in my life. There was a time where I decided to resign from my place of employment without a plan or vision in place as to what would be next in my life. After a few days of feeling empty, discouraged and confused, it was within my spirit to seek God in a way that I have never attempted in times past. I said to myself, "Jackie, what are you going to do differently?" It was then, where I decided to go on a fast and consecration. There was one day, where I was listening to a podcast entitled "David's Oil" by Apostle Bryan Meadows, and from taking notes, receiving the word in my spirit, it was then that the Holy Spirit spoke to me.

I was asking the Lord to show me the real thing inside of me that is hindering growth, hindering me from progressing, and hindering me in ministry. Lord, why did I do that? I believe sometimes we ask God questions but are not prepared to receive an answer from Him quickly.

The spirit immediately spoke to me and said "You have a history of giving up too early and too easy. The reason being is because you do not want to take ownership of who YOU ARE in me. He says to me "You are running from everything that is for you because you cannot be in control and because you don't have the knowledge of it all. You are doing it (life and ministry) without me (God) and trying to compromise within yourself to get what you want, or think is right. You are everything that you deny to others and to yourself. You must override fear and lack of knowledge and move forward in faith, staying connected to me (God). You can't do it without me and need my guidance every step of the way."

My brothers and sisters, I begin weeping uncontrollably after hearing the spirit of the Lord speak these words to me. It made so much sense as to why in my life the struggles, the challenges, hardships, and other pressures of life were weighing on me. Primarily because of running from what God wanted to do in my life and how He wanted me to be confident in every spiritual gift, anointing, and ministry work that lies on the inside of me. From that place, I began a journey of daily prayers and intercession with the Lord. God began to deal with my inner man. The more He dealt with my heart, mind and spirit in prayer, the more I confessed my faults to Him. God begin to remove layers, tear down barricades, pull out issues from the root to bring me into deliverance. The Lord begin taking me deeper into His presence and my hunger for him grew stronger. This book entails some of my most intimate prayer experiences with God during this time, as He took me on a journey to heal my inner man, build relationship with Him, provide me with tools in prayer and now I am able to be a PRAYER AGENT for His kingdom.

Prayer and Intercession has been embedded in me since I was a child. I recall growing up in the Church of God in Christ (COGIC), attending shut-ins, and prayer services where most times, I was the only kid in attendance. Prayer became my lifeline at a very young age. It was prayer that was released from my lips as a child that brought salvation to my family. THANK YOU, JESUS. The older I was getting; the more prayer grew with me. Funny thing is, I was not formally trained in prayer or attended a prayer class, workshop, or conference until my young adult years. However, the Holy Spirit trained me in prayer by simply putting a cry inside of me and a trust in who God is. Of course, as a child, you mimic what you see from the older saints, but I was not one of those children. I have always had a distinctive way on how I would seek God in prayer and was sure that my way of speaking with Him was my own way.

In my early 20s, I attended a Wednesday night Bible class at Mt. Calvary Baptist Church. The Pastor's wife, Lady Regina Crider, came to me, laid her hands on my stomach and said to me "I want you to pray tonight. I know there is prayer stored up inside of this belly." As hesitant as I was and confused as to how she knew that prayer was inside of me, I approached the microphone and something forceful erupted from my belly. Today, I laugh about it, because it was so explosive that I do not recall what was coming out of me. The Lord took over the service that night in a mighty way. I was so honored that He chose me to be anointed to release prayer during that hour. From that day, Lady Regina Crider became my spiritual mentor who through the leading of the Lord, trained me deeply in prayer and intercession. Lady Regina Crider is one of God's mouthpieces as it pertains to prayer and intercession. I truly admire her for taking the time to develop and pull out what lies inside of me.

As my journey continued in life pertaining to prayer and intercession, there were times God would anoint me in the workplace to offer prayer for co-workers, managers and supervisors.

With that being said, I am a strong advocate for pushing prayer in every place, for every person, and in everything. A prayer agent is what I am, and for this movement to take place beyond my zeal, desire and passion for prayer, it is IMPERATIVE that more prayer agents are birthed out.

<u>Introduction</u>

· Where do I begin in prayer?

· I am not familiar with prayer; how do I learn?

· How do I regain my passion back for prayer?

· I have been praying this way for years, now what?

· What is the difference between prayer and intercession?

· How do I know God hears me when I pray?

Many Christian believers and new converts have asked themselves some of these questions on their walk with God. Prayer can be the one area that causes people to change their view on their relationship with God based upon what is being displayed in front of them. Prayer inside the local church can often times make you feel as if you have to possess a certain vocal ability or style, extensive vocabulary, accomplished the highest degree in education, and have obtained the greatest title in ministry in order to pray effectively. Sometimes in the church it can feel as if without certain criteria or stylistic delivery, your prayer can be deemed ineffective.

Although there are numerous reasons why individuals are hindered from obtaining an active and effective prayer life, I want to highlight a few common areas.

· **<u>Denomination or Religion:</u>** A person may have become conditioned to the ritualistic prayer activity within a certain denomination or religious practice. This likely results in a hindered prayer life if the person finds it difficult to operate in prayer beyond what has been taught or is protocol. This is often found to lead to a not so pleasant experience resulting in a disconnection to prayer. If a person's upbringing in prayer was in the Catholic church for example, or a part of Jehovah's witness, one may find it challenging to adjust to the Christian way of prayer.

· **<u>How one was raised in prayer</u>**: Where were you groomed, trained, and developed in prayer? Who taught you how to pray? Many people who do not have an active prayer life likely were not trained/developed in prayer or were taught to pray in simplistic form such as the famous "before bed" prayer, "Now I lay me down to sleep, I pray the Lord my soul to keep…" Most of us are familiar with that prayer and the prayer of grace before eating a meal. I call those "surface level" prayers. The great news is, for children, it establishes a connection with God and places a prayer in the mind that is redundant and easy to recite verbatim. These surface prayers can reside within an individual for generations to come. However, as you mature in God, so should your prayer life and relationship with him mature.

· **Lack of knowledge in the word of God:** The Bible can often feel intimidating and challenging to understand with all the variety of names, cultures, genealogies, and languages that are difficult to pronounce and digest. Some people have said, "I read the word and I get nothing out of it." As a matter of fact, when I read the word of God, I get very sleepy. Have you ever felt like that? The enemy is seeking during that time of study to sabotage and hijack our thoughts so that we do not absorb the revelation of the word. What happens when we are not confident and diligent readers of the word? Simply put, it leads to an inactive prayer life. The word of God is NEEDED and NECESSARY in your ability to articulate effective communication to the Lord in prayer.

· **Lack of communication skills**: How one communicates with people here on earth is a determining factor in your communication with God. If you are one who has trouble conveying your innermost true feelings to those you encounter on a regular basis, then prayer could be a challenge for you as well. If you are a person who expresses very little dialogue to others, keeps everything on the inside and are non- confrontational, then prayer will be uncomfortable for you. A good amount of people who build up a case against themselves and exhibit these behaviors, rely on others who do not have these characteristics to pray for them. Do not get me wrong, we are to be helpers one to another as well as to strengthen our brothers and sisters in times of weakness. However, the Lord has equipped all of us, introverts and extroverts, to be able to seek Him for whatever we need, establish a communication with Him, and to get the results needed in the earth.

· **<u>Lack of relational skills</u>**: For those who have the challenge of "showing yourself friendly" in obtaining friends and those who lack healthy relationships could find prayer a challenge. Individuals who have that "I don't need anything or anyone" attitude will find it hard to connect with God in general as well as in prayer. Relational skills require some of the following: Honesty, Trust, transparency, love, giving of oneself, standing the test of time through hardships, ability to agree when you disagree and more. Those who lack healthy earthly relationships will treat their prayer life, and God just the same.

<u>Moment of Reflection</u>

What are my prayer blockers?

Can you relate to any of these prayer blockers? If so, make note below.

· _____: Could be (or is) a reflection of the area of lack in my personal prayer life.

How will you obtain healing in this area for the development of a stronger prayer life?

_____

_____

_____

_____

_____

_____

_____

_____

_____

_____

_____

_____

_____

_____

God never intended for your prayer life to be a complete resemblance of someone else's. Prayer has weight, rank, dimensions, realms, various destinations, which never stops. Prayer is a capacity that cannot be measured, limited, confined, or remain stagnant. Prayer, when released properly, causes results, releases answers, provides direction from the Lord, and interrupts the plans of the enemy. Prayer is a hunger, a burden, and a thirst that is being craved from the soul of an individual seeking connection with the Father.

For example: During pregnancy, the child inside of the woman becomes in control. The woman carrying the child was able to eat what she wanted, sleep how she desired, dressed in the form fitting clothes of choice prior to becoming pregnant.

During the various trimesters of a pregnancy, the woman will experience different changes within their body depending on what they are carrying. Changes such as nausea, shortness of breath, body form change, swelling in the feet, sensitivity to smell, vomiting, constant sickness etc. Pregnant women are NOT all the same. Nor will they experience the exact same symptoms nor have the same gender or quantity of children as the next woman. The only thing pregnant women have in common is that there is a change/adjustment in their lives, a seed has been planted, and there is a projected plan for delivery.

Let me encourage you, prayer contains that same type of feeling and works the same way. As we establish a healthy relationship of prayer in God, He impregnates us with His word and a new dialect and dialogue, that empowers us to identify our unique voice pattern in prayer. Do you hear me?

In God, you have a distinctive voice pattern like no one else, and God knows you according to that voice pattern, sound, diction, vocabulary and more. It is millions upon millions of people in the world, yet in God, He gives everyone their own way of communicating with Him.

Have you ever noticed when babies are born throughout this world, that not one of them is completely identical to the next? There are times where babies, children, and adults, favor each other very closely but still not the same. God created His people to always have a distinctive identity.

Same applies to prayer for the people of God. When you pray, the Lord wants you to pray like He designed you and not like anyone else. There are no carbon copies in Christ Jesus.

It is good to attend training on prayer and follow a mentor, but your purpose in connecting is for you to receive the content. Upon completing those trainings, it is then for God to take what is inside of you, connect it with the content and birth out of you what He desires.

Let me help you with this. The position, posture and assignment of prayer that is on your life comes with its own warfare, demonic oppositions, discernment, and more. Do not be a seed stealer, be a recipient of receiving seeds and plant them as God instructs. In the word of God, Solomon was brought into a fiasco with two women claiming to be the mother of a child. Look at what happened:

16 Then two women who were prostitutes came to the king and stood before him. 17 And the one woman said, "O my lord, this woman and I live in the same house; and I gave birth to a child while she was in the house. 18 And on the third day after I gave birth, this woman also gave birth. And we were [alone] together; no one else was with us in the house, just we two. 19 Now this woman's son died during the night, because she lay on him [and smothered him]. 20 So she got up in the middle of the night and took my son from [his place] beside me while your maidservant was asleep, and laid him on her bosom, and laid her dead son on my bosom. 21 When I got up in the morning to nurse my son, behold, he was dead. But when I examined him carefully in the morning, behold, it was not my son, the one whom I had borne." 22 Then the other woman said, "No! For my son is the one who is living, and your son is the dead one." But the first woman said, "No! For your son is the dead one, and my son is the living one." [This is how] they were speaking before the king.

23 Then the king said, "This woman says, 'This is my son, the one who is alive, and your son is the dead one'; and the other woman says, 'No! For your son is the dead one, and my son is the one who is alive.'" 24 Then the king said, "Bring me a sword." So, they brought a sword before the king. 25 Then the king said, "Cut the living child in two, and give half to the one [woman] and half to the other." 26 Then the woman whose child was the living one spoke to the king, for she was deeply moved over her son, "O my lord, give her the living child, and by no means kill him." But the other said, "He shall be neither mine nor yours; cut him!" 27 Then the king said, "Give the first woman [who is pleading for his life] the living child, and by no means kill him. She is his mother."

-1 Kings 3:16-27-AMP

What an amazing story of what happens when you seek to take possession of something that does not belong to you. The women came to the wisest man ever created to convince him to decide on who the child belongs to. After Solomon made it clear to make the most drastic decision, the birth mother released a desperate cry that got the attention of Solomon's spirit as she was more connected to the child. Understand this, what you work for in God as it pertains to your spiritual gifts, prayer life, connection with God, you should be so protective of it that you will not allow anyone or anything to take it from you. Understand? God has planted seed of righteousness inside of you that is worth fighting and standing for. Not to be easily released into the hands of others. Brothers and sisters, decree and declare confidence over your ability to pray. It is the time to get pregnant in God, allowing him to seed you. There will be no abortions or miscarriages in this season of your life, but you will carry full term until your point of delivery. IN JESUS's NAME. Here are two terms prayer agents should become familiar with:

Intercession:

The time of entrance, interception, and carrying.

Intercession can be described as the womb of the prayer as it is incubated and birthed from this place. However, intercession is not something only promised to some. Although it has its own identity in the way that it is manifested, it is the same "action" for all. The change in identity here comes from the difference in the womb that carries it, not in the sense that intercession itself has different identities.

Intercession causes you to interrupt (intercept) whatever the enemy planned to accomplish. Just as in sports, when the opposing team makes a pass to a fellow team mate to score a point, a player from the opposite team attempts to jump in and cause interruption in the play. The intercessor watches, observes, sounds the alarm and puts a plan of action in place QUICKLY so that the attack will NOT succeed.

Deliverance: The point of birthing, bringing forth, transition into the new.

Prayer will push you from intercession to deliverance. In this stage you see the result of what you have been praying for manifest in a new way. During the intercession period you may not see exactly what you're praying or interceding for, but you feel it and know that it's there. You feel the contractions and labor pains but at the point of delivery, you release the thing that you been carrying all this time. When praying, it is so important that we become and remain open and vulnerable. Prayer is not designed to be self-focused on one's personal earthly gain.

When entering prayer, it becomes about communing with the Father, connecting with his Will, speaking and listening to Him. Prayer is not about the time limit. One who prays for 10 hours a day, verses one who prays 10 minutes per day does not make the prayer time effective or yield a greater result. The time spent with God becomes effective when it's coming from the heart, spirit and soul of a person who just wants to commune with God.

41 And He sat down opposite the [temple] treasury and began watching how the people were putting money into the [l]treasury. And many rich people were putting in [m]large sums. 42 A poor widow came and put in two small copper coins, which amount to a [n]mite. 43 Calling His disciples to Him, He said to them, "I assure you and most solemnly say to you, this poor widow put in [proportionally] more than all the contributors to the treasury. 44 For they all contributed from their surplus, but she, from her poverty, put in all she had, all she had to live on."

- Mark 12: 41-44 AMP

Jesus, watching the people give their money, was not moved by how much was given monetarily but more from the spirit. What moved God was not just the money the widow woman gave but the spirit in which she gave it. What am I saying? You can be well versed and trained to pray for hours but, if the purpose of your prayer is based upon traditionalism, redundant behaviors and lack of His spirit, then it is not moving God. Extensive time communicating with God is important to Him when your heart, spirit, mind, and body coupled with faith is involved. Making prayer a priority is one that each prayer agent should aim to incorporate daily. Hear me, not just the "act" of prayer but the hunger, passion, desire, in seeking to connect with Him daily. Prayer agents should develop the "such as I have given I thee" mentality from the Apostle Peter found in Acts 3:6.

The Bible says it like this in **Hebrews 11:6** KJV **But** without faith it is impossible to please him: for he that cometh to God must believe that he is, and that he is a rewarder of them that diligently seek him.

The key word in this scripture is "IMPOSSIBLE". Basically, what is being stated is with God, who specializes in the impossible, can only move on those who have faith in Him. If there is doubt or negativity in the purposed plan and promised word from God, then He sits still releasing nothing. WOW! Here is why when we pray and faith is activated in our prayers, that He responds to us. Faith must be the anchor in every prayer we release to God. It takes faith to pray to the Father because we often do not know what to pray for, but we take the chance anyway just to seek Him. When we pray, we are unsure of what the Lord will say, accept, or reject but we go to Him anyway. Just as children who wants something from their parents, you never know what the answer will be that comes out of their mouths but, because you want it so bad

you take the chance to inquire. Regardless of the answer the parent will give you, the courage comes in when you take the risk (faith activation) and ask.
Allow yourself to be open, find the best environment and time frame in which you can communicate with God uninterrupted.

Prayer Agents, are you ready to take the world with the word of God, for the kingdom of God?

Prayer Agents by Jackie A. Jones Jr.

Prayer Agents by Jackie A. Jones Jr.

Part I

Strengthen the Inner Man

In order to be a prayer agent, you must be willing to possess the following criteria:

○   Ready to reproduce a generation

○   Willing to do the work on oneself internally and externally

○   Have the mindset of seeking God's presence diligently

○   Adapt to speaking the language of the kingdom

○   Clear out the gates of your life: eye, ear, mouth, nose, and mind

Strengthening the inner man requires work being done on the inside of the vessel. As the scripture describes in 2 Corinthians 4:7: *"We have this treasure in earthen vessels,* many times we are unable to tap into this treasure due to the hindrances that cause us to be blocked from who God has called us to be. We are often told that we have anointing, oil, and power, but if I can offer this suggestion, it is very possible we are unlearned and unknowledgeable about what these terms really mean.

The Bible puts it like this in **Hosea 4:6 AMP**: *My people are destroyed for lack of knowledge [of My law, where I reveal My will]. Because you [the priestly nation] have rejected knowledge.*

The best example I can give to describe the treasure inside of us, is the process of the olive.

The olive process is one that is necessary and needed in the body of Christ. The oil flows from the olive when it is crushed and burned, not when it's hanging on a tree. The process of extracting the oil from the olive begins with a washing, a tearing, followed by a burning and crushing. Immediately after the crushing, the oil is released and endures a purifying which then leads to being packaged for a purpose.

Oftentimes we want to remain on the tree to avoid the process and skip right to releasing oil. Therefore, allowing other olives to fall and be processed while we are stagnant, complacent just being an olive. But soon, Jesus will curse the tree that is not bearing fruit.

He will find a way to remove that olive which can cause it to either become useless or He will force it to enter the crushing/burning process against its will. A tree that does not produce is cursed. Let us look to the word of God for reference.

"Mark 11:13-14 AMP – [12] On the next day, when they had left Bethany, He was hungry. [13] Seeing at a distance a fig tree in leaf, He went to see if He would find anything on it. But He found nothing but leaves, for it was not the season for figs. [14] He said to it, "No one will ever eat fruit from you again!""

In this scripture you find that Jesus came to the tree with an expectation that it was serving its purpose which was productivity. The visual of the tree lets us know that seeds were planted in the ground. This further suggests that time was taken to establish a tree that would produce. The fact that Jesus approached the manifestation of a tree set to produce fruit and found nothing, was not pleasing in His sight. What are you saying Jackie? I am simply saying you were seeded and planted to produce! The purpose of God creating you was for you to produce as a conduit that channels what is in heaven down to the earth. How does Jesus view you when He approaches your tree? Have you endured being an olive longer than you needed to? What is on your tree? Are you producing?

God wants what is on the inside of you to come out. Although there may be many olives on a tree with the same shape, same color, same roles of responsibility, there is still something unique about each olive. The process of extracting the oil from the olive is the same.

However, there is a value inside of each olive that the Lord desires to use for his glory. Prayer will pull the oil out of you in a way you could never imagine. The oil inside of you is utilized to destroy yokes of bondage, demonic strongholds, and release heaven on earth. It is time for you to move from the tree! It is time for you to fall to the ground, endure the crushing, go through the burning, and release the oil.

Isaiah 43:2 KJV is God's reassurance for this process:

²When thou passest through the waters, I will be with thee; and through the rivers, they shall not overflow thee: when thou walkest through the fire, thou shalt not be burned; neither shall the flame kindle upon thee. Amazing right? He is saying to you, that during this time of self-denial, consecration, and transparency, I…AM…. WITH…. YOU!! GOD is saying, I GOT YOU COVERED.

Wow, what an awesome God we serve. God is saying this to share His heart with you and encourage you during the process. Yes, it may hurt, it may sting, it may seem like so much pressure is on your shoulders. However, the Lord is saying it is a necessary process that is going to yield a greater result and establish the properly aligned connection with him.

Strengthen the mind

The mind is the place where the enemy loves to attack. It is in the mind where some of the greatest warfare takes place. What you do not see in the natural begins to tell your mind, whatever the Lord promised will not manifest.

Romans 8:24-25 KJV says it like this;
For we are saved by hope: but hope that is seen is not hope: for what a man seeth, why doth he yet hope for? But if we hope for that we see not, then do we with patience wait for it.

If we only have hope based upon what we see, then where is the miracle in that? The Lord wants us to have hope in the things we do NOT see so that what He does in the spirit will astound us at the time of manifestation. The Bible says we are "transformed by the renewing of our mind" (**Romans 12:2 KJV)** and that He is "able to do ABOVE what we ask or think." (**Ephesians 3:20 KJV).**

This is your ammunition to use in prayer. You must have understanding that you are placed in a seat of authority.

The Bible says in **Ephesians 2:6-AMP** "And He raised us up together with Him [when we believed], and seated us with Him in the heavenly places, [because we are] in Christ Jesus, [7] [and He did this] so that in the ages to come He might [clearly] show the immeasurable and unsurpassed riches of His grace in [His] kindness toward us in Christ Jesus [by providing for our redemption].

Therefore, my thinking as a prayer agent has left its seat of authority and has descended to a low place when I experience disappointment, frustration, and anger about life's circumstances on earth. This causes us to operate in a manner that is out of character. Do not get me wrong, as humans in this Christian walk, we will experience trouble, persecution, heartaches and more. However, it becomes a concern when we dwell on the problem longer than intended. The more we feed the problem with negativity the more we come into agreement with the emotional instability and oblige the sin.

God can take care of every bill, every issue, and every problem. Elevate your mind into the Kingdom mindset! Come back and be seated. Set your mind on things above according to Colossians 2:3. It is not by accident that your mind was not created and placed in your feet. It was placed in the highest posture of the human anatomy for a reason. By this it can always be an indicator that you are to always be positioned upward, on top, and in control. The enemy wants to attack the mind for that same reason. The head is the place of authority. If the enemy can attack the headship of authority, detour your thoughts and manipulate you from that authoritative place, then he has accomplished his task. THE DEVIL IS A LIAR! Your mind shall be solid and strong!

Philippians 2:5 KJV "Let this mind be in you, which was also in Christ Jesus.

Do you see the authority in this scripture? It begins with the word "LET" meaning to not prevent or forbid but to allow. The scripture does not begin with the proposition of asking permission but it commands. It goes on to say Let this mind! Who is mind? THIS MIND be in you which is also in Christ Jesus. Prayer agents I urge you to call your mind into its rightful, destined and designed place. Demand your mind to get in order and alignment with God.

<u>Strengthen the Heart</u>

As prayer agents, it is super important that we work on our hearts. When we pray, we seek the heart of God and He is so gracious, merciful and kind to share His heart with those who seek Him.

Jeremiah 29:13-AMP says it like this: [13] Then [with a deep longing] you will seek Me and require Me [as a vital necessity] and [you will] find Me when you search for Me with all your heart.

The Lord says, when you seek me with your whole heart, you will find me. The heart is one of the strongest organs in the human body. In prayer, if we are not willing to offer up our whole heart to the Lord, it is going to be very challenging to reach Him and receive from Him.

Let us explore the anatomy of the heart to gauge a better perspective on its function:

Research states that the heart has neurons which is basically like a brain. The signals from the heart goes to the other parts of the body, especially the brain. The brain takes its direction from the heart. If the heart sends something, then it is already validated as law. Neurons send signals using action potentials. An action potential is a shift in the neuron's electric potential caused by the flow of ions in and out of the neural membrane. Once the mind receives the message, the mind goes to work. When the mind goes to work, there is then a reaction be it outwardly expression, or thoughts that will attract the very thing that is established and received.

What is fascinating is that the heart contains a little brain. Yes, the human heart, in addition to its other functions, possesses a heart-brain composed of about 40,000 neurons that can sense, feel, learn and remember.

The heart is closely linked to the brain. It is linked so much that it is constantly sending information to it and even activating and inhibiting various areas of the brain depending on certain bodily needs.

You might like to know, for example, that emotions like love – as well as its manifestation through affection, tenderness, and care – come from this exceptional complex of cells, nerves, energy, and electricity that make up who we are. We are perfectly engineered to interact with our environment and fellow humans.

Your heart sends far more signals to your brain, than your brain sends to your heart. The heart is in a constant two-way dialog with the brain. Our emotions change the signals that the brain sends to the heart and the heart responds in complex ways. The brain has 100 billion neurons while the heart has 40,000.

WOW! That is a lot to take in right? You ask me, what does this have to do with being a prayer agent, well my brothers and sisters, I am so glad you asked me that question.

The Lord begin to share a deeper revelation regarding the heart with me and how we harbor of it knowingly and unknowingly. Imagine you were three years old, and your parent(s) walked out on you. Immediately, what happened at that point of your life was rejection, abandonment, guilt, resentment, and possibly more.

It has been 30 years, and still there has not been any communication or reuniting with that parent(s). What tends to happen for those who have never been released from that three-year-old child suffering from that loss, is unforgiveness has built up and it went into a place within the heart. I hear people sometimes, say oh yeah, I've gotten over that and moved on but I have to say, if untreated, or not addressed, this has grown up inside of you and according to many of your behaviors it's exuding from you. What occurs is, the individual who has not treated this issue or problem is either aware or unaware of their behaviors towards themselves as well as others in their lives. Untreated heart issues can cause an individual to become numb in their life, comfortable in their behaviors, and put up walls, barriers, and distrust towards anyone who genuinely wants to love them as well as them loving themselves. Interesting right?!

As you are growing with this untreated emotion in your heart, it sends this to your brain cells over and over again. So your brain is saying, "don't trust him or her", "they are taking advantage of you", "this person will leave you just like your parent did", so then you end up building up a false case against people who come into your life based upon the pain that is in your heart and either reject good people or attract people to you who exhibit what that parent did to you. Again, this happens knowingly and unknowingly. The heart must be cleaned, purified, detoxed so that you can be fully healed from every occurrence in your life that left a void there. See, in prayer your heart reveals, exposes, and confronts the truth which is why the enemy (inner me), will cause an individual to have surface prayers. Surface prayers is what I call, "just enough to get by". Praying when you are saying your grace, or just saying "Thank you Lord" for waking you up, or the famous "Now I lay me down to sleep" prayers.

God desires that we go deeper into prayer where our heart reaches His heart and He reveal, shares, releases, heals, delivers and manifest his glory. The challenge is being willing to go all the way.

The word of God says this about the heart:
Proverbs 23:7 KJV "For as he thinketh in his heart, so is he."

Jeremiah 17:9-10 Message Bible

"The heart is hopelessly dark and deceitful, a puzzle that no one can figure out.
But I, God, search the heart and examine the mind.
I get to the heart of the human. I get to the root of things.
I treat them as they really are, not as they pretend to be."

Proverbs 4:23 NIV

Above all else, guard your heart, for everything you do flows from it.

Psalms 147:3 KJV

"He healeth the broken in heart, and bindeth up their wounds."

These scriptures help us to identify the state our heart is in. For some of us we are close to Proverbs 23:7, which suggests why we react the way we do, and/or where our confidence level is within ourselves. This is a heart issue that needs to be addressed and the Lord can reveal that to you in prayer. Others may relate to Jeremiah 17:9-10, as there are many things occurring in the heart but are unable to pinpoint exactly what they are. But God, searches the heart and He knows specifically what is there and can deliver. In prayer this is a time where you are transparent with him and allow him to detox the hidden secrets, hidden warfare, hidden emotions, and blockage that lies deep within. A few of you may be in a place like Proverbs 4:23 where you have not guarded your heart and allowed your issues to flow out before you had a chance to stop it from coming out. Whew! I call this giving your heart away to any and everyone due to vulnerability, lack of wisdom and understanding. However, God can step in and put a guard over your heart, provide you with the wisdom you need to filter into your heart what is healthy versus what's damaging.

As you can see, prayer affects and impacts the heart of the believer. If your heart is healthy, so will your prayer life become. Once prayer is in your heart, you receive strength, wisdom, knowledge, revelation, and tap into the mysteries of God. When God enters your heart, everything else that is not like him MUST be removed. I admonish you to release your heart to the Lord, apply the word of God inside of your heart that you MIGHT NOT sin against him.

<u>Strengthen the Body</u>

Prayer requires full submission to the Lord. Prayer agents should be prepared for the following:

- Denial of the flesh
- The breaking of self-pride
- Disengage from emotions
- Consistent intimacy with God.

Sounds like a lot of self-evaluation, right? I want to offer this concept as it pertains to the body. Married couples who are intimate on a consistent and consecutive basis, can run into the possibility of getting pregnant. When you discover after many sexual encounters, you are now pregnant, there is a decision to be made. The question arises "Should we proceed with maintaining the pregnancy or not?".

Where am I going with this? I am glad you asked!
1 Corinthians 6:19-20 (NIV) [9] Do you not know that your bodies are temples of the Holy Spirit, who is in you, whom you have received from God? You are not your own; [20] you were bought at a price. Therefore, honor God with your bodies.

When you worship the Lord, seek Him in prayer, or just connect with Him in the spirit, He fills you and impregnates you. When you return to sin, you run the risk of aborting the seed that has been planted within you. Returning to sin opens the door to embracing the territory, energy, and demonic forces associated with that sin for your life. It will then hinder your prayer life, worship lifestyle and connection with God.

Matthew 12:43-45-AMP: [43] "Now when the unclean spirit has gone out of a man, it roams through waterless (dry, arid) places in search of rest, but it does not find it. [44] Then it says, 'I will return to my house from which I came.' And when it arrives, it finds the place unoccupied, swept, and put in order. [45] Then it goes and brings with it seven other spirits more wicked than itself, and they go in and make their home there. And the last condition of that man becomes worse than the first. So will it also be with this wicked generation."

When God puts seed inside of you, that seed has the power to drive out demonic forces causing them to no longer take residence on the inside of you. The more you pray, you are watering and nurturing that seed and it begins to grow. The sin that was once removed, waits until you provide an opening, then comes back with seven other spirits and takes residence on the inside of you. The moment you turn back to sin, allowing it inside of your womb, there becomes the wheat and the tear growing together.

It is as if you are now watering two seeds at the same time and there is a war happening with good and evil. What you find happening is both seeds are seeking to discover who will be nurtured the most and who will win this battle. There becomes a battle of nations in the womb just like Jacob and Esau in **Genesis 25:21-24.**

It is so important that prayer agents continue to submit your bodies unto the Lord. Protect the seed on the inside of you giving no room for the enemy to dwell and take residence.

Prayer agents are responsible for operating in seedtime and harvest continually in our lives. We have the power to reject the spirit of the abortionist and provide spiritual support to the womb causing miscarriages not to occur. Your spiritual body was created by God to be a womb, always carrying seed until the time and season of delivery. We will look more closely at prayers that bring deliverance in Part III.

One way to constantly strengthen your body and the inner man is found in the book of Jude.

Jude 1:20 KJV: But ye, beloved, building up yourselves on your most holy faith, praying in the Holy Ghost.

Praying in the Holy Ghost, your heavenly language keeps you strong. The Lord provided you with a gift, and with that gift you are talking straight to the Lord and no one else. Isn't that great news!? We have a tool, a power, a language that can be interpreted by the Holy Spirit and it says to Him exactly what English words, cannot interpret or express for us.

BUILDING A RELATIONSHIP WITH GOD

I recall a time where I invited a new convert (new to Christianity) out to a prayer service a few years ago. She was excited about this new season of her life. She was never really into attending prayer service until I extended an invitation. During the service, the spirit of the Lord took over and it was an amazing experience. As the service concluded, I went to find her, and she was in tears. I assumed they were tears of joy in the spirit of God. Boy was I wrong! She was hysterical! This experience left her feeling so undervalued, embarrassed and ashamed that she attended this service and was not educated on how to pray. She felt alone, isolated and overlooked. She expressed how most of those attending the service was fluent in speaking in tongues, knowledgeable on how to pray for others, and advanced in prayer. Little did she know, it was quite a few people in the room who felt just as she did. However, I began to encourage her because I did not want her to be angry with herself and disconnect from God. Understanding the environment was intimidating and uncomfortable, God has given us all a unique, distinctive prayer language and style. That conversation is what prompted me to write this book because I know there are so many people who feel the same as she did. Having the fear-based thoughts such as;

- I cannot pray
- I am uneducated in prayer
- God does not hear me
- I am useless and powerless in prayer

One of the reasons, the enemy puts those thoughts in the mind, is to hinder a person from tapping into the power of God THROUGH prayer. Prayer grants us access into the unknown.

Ephesians 3:12 Amplified Bible (AMP): **12** in whom we have boldness and confident access through faith in Him [that is, our faith gives us sufficient courage to freely and openly approach God through Christ].

When we come to God, we enter His presence (*grabs his attention*), make our request known, and we create an exchange between us and Him.

A few steps that takes place in building a relationship with another person are:

- Establishing a set way of communicating with one another
- Gaining insight on the other individual
- Discover similarities with one another
- Spend time with the individual to understand likes and dislikes
- Learn the history and family dynamic of the individual

There are many more active steps that leads to creating and building relationship with someone. Just as we take necessary steps to learn our spouses, children, friends and family, it is just the same with God. Look at this scripture in Matthew 7:21-23 as it pertains to what Jesus says regarding connection/relationship:

Matthew 7:21-23 KJV: [21] Not everyone that saith unto me, Lord, shall enter into the kingdom of heaven; but he that doeth the will of my Father which is in heaven. Many will say to me in that day, Lord, Lord, have we not prophesied in thy name? and in thy name have cast out devils? and in thy name done many wonderful works? And then will I profess unto them, I never knew you: depart from me, ye that work iniquity.

Knowing Jesus requires spending time with Him, living according to the word of God, staying connected to Him at all cost, right? Jesus desires that we have relationship with Him as He takes pleasure in being the Lord over our lives. The Lord enjoys being the provider, the healer and the deliverer for His people. YES LORD!

Know this, having good morals, being active in your community, being active in the church, and doing good deeds in the world, does not equate to a relationship with God. Although, these deeds are honorable, and respectful, if you do not have (as the scripture says in John 15:4-7) "the Father and the Father does not live within you", then it only validates good works. I believe the Lord blesses those who bless His people, but I also believe when you have relationship with Him there is more abundance that is released. Consider this, one who gives to the poor at random or even with a strategy without the leading of the Lord is doing what is right. Great Job! Can you imagine one who gives to the poor because the Lord said so? That would be fulfilling a command that God wanted to be done at that specific time. For example, the Lord may say give the poor one thousand dollars, food baskets, and clothing. Sounds like a lot! But, the reaping of blessing is when you have completed the assignment for the Lord, He then sends a monetary blessing back to you that you could have never imagined! God is not a lottery machine, gypsy or a good luck charm. We are not blessing people with the sole purpose of getting something back.

However, we want to be so sensitive to His voice that we obey His instruction doing what He wants, how He wants it done. All of this will be revealed when you establish a life of prayer with God. We move beyond "good deeds and works" into kingdom fulfillment. That is the place we want to be.

As a prayer agent, you will not be effective, powerful, or useful in the spiritual things of God without relationship with the Father.

Building a Relationship with Faith in God (Belief vs Unbelief)

Faith builds your trust with God. If God can see your faith, then He will be able to trust you with His assignments.

We will look more closely at prayer assignments in Part II.

God is moved by faith which involves trust and belief. When there is unbelief, there becomes lack of movement as God only responds by the faith within His people.

 Unbelief hinders Him from moving, operating and blessing the way He intends to. According to the word of God here are two examples of belief and unbelief:

Mark Chapter 5:2-6 KJV: And when he was come out of the ship, immediately there met him out of the tombs a man with an unclean spirit, Who had his dwelling among the tombs; and no man could bind him, no, not with chains:[4] Because that he had been often bound with fetters and chains, and the chains had been plucked asunder by him, and the fetters broken in pieces: neither could any man tame him. And always, night and day, he was in the mountains, and in the tombs, crying, and cutting himself with stones. But when he saw Jesus afar off, he ran and worshipped him.

This passage of scripture deals with quite a few areas that we can unpack. First, you have a man possessed with demons tormenting him day and night. This man was heavily bound by these evil forces that no one could hold him down. In addition to him being bound by demonic forces, he dealt with the spirit of suicide as he was cutting himself with stones.

I would imagine the mindset of this man was in a place of confusion, anger, frustration, and mental instability. However, during all that was occurring with him, the Bible says he sees Jesus afar off. Wait a minute, his mind, body, and spirit were shambolic, but his vision was still intact. So much so, that when he saw Jesus he ran and worshipped him. What would cause a demonic possessed man to run towards Jesus and worship Him? It was the spirit of faith inside of the man who was bound that saw relief and deliverance in Jesus. Therefore, causing the man to alienate what he was going through to get to Jesus.

We must believe in God, even when we are in situations that have us so bound, that it seems there is no way out. Amazing how a man whose being tormented day and night and cutting himself, stayed alive long enough to receive his deliverance. It was not only the faith inside of him still going strong, but I believe prayer agents were on assignment praying on his behalf!

Let us look at the form of unbelief from **Luke 9:37-43 NIV**

[37] The next day, when they came down from the mountain, a large crowd met him. [38] A man in the crowd called out, "Teacher, I beg you to look at my son, for he is my only child. [39] A spirit seizes him and he suddenly screams; it throws him into convulsions so that he foams at the mouth. It scarcely ever leaves him and is destroying him. [40] I begged your disciples to drive it out, but they could not."

[41] "You unbelieving and perverse generation," Jesus replied, "how long shall I stay with you and put up with you? Bring your son here."

[42] Even while the boy was coming, the demon threw him to the ground in a convulsion. But Jesus rebuked the impure spirit, healed the boy and gave him back to his father. [43] And they were all amazed at the greatness of God.

Jesus was straightforward with His disciples. The disciples were walking with Jesus for most of His great miracles, healings, teachings, encounters and experiences. Connecting with Jesus was a time of receiving wise counsel, instruction and order in the spirit. But there were times where even those closest to Him operated in unbelief. Here is a prime example of a demonic manifestation occurring and the disciples could not cast it out due to unbelief. Jesus had to handle it Himself!

God wants to be pleased therefore when He is not pleased, it shows. Unbelief says there is doubt and possibly even fear in executing the plan of God.

Look at how faith is ignited and can shift quickly to unbelief:

11 "Now [the meaning of] the parable is this: The seed is the word of God [concerning eternal salvation]. 12 Those beside the road are the people who have heard; then the devil comes and takes the message [of God] away from their hearts, so that they will not believe [in Me as the Messiah] and be saved. 13 Those on the rocky soil are the people who, when they hear, receive and welcome the word with joy; but these have no firmly grounded root. They believe for a while, and in time of trial and temptation they fall away [from Me and abandon their faith]. 14 The seed which fell among the thorns, these are the ones who have heard, but as they go on their way they are suffocated with the anxieties and riches and pleasures of this life, and they bring no fruit to maturity. 15 But as for that seed in the good soil, these are the ones who have heard the word with a good and noble heart, and hold on to it tightly, and bear fruit with patience.

- Luke 8:11-15-Amplified Version

When the word of God enters your heart, it then ignites your faith in God. The enemy knows that if the word gets inside of your heart and remain there, you will not be swayed or swindled by what you see or hear. Ultimately causing you to be steadfast, unmovable always abounding in the work of the Lord. **1 Corinthians 15:58**. The word of God resting, abiding in the heart of an individual is a threat to the enemy as he is not ignorant concerning the word of God. Jeremiah 32:37 says: And I will give them one heart, and one way, that they may fear me forever, for the good of them, and of their children after them."

It is the job of the enemy to use every tactic he possibly can to remove the word of God from your heart. The enemy wants you to shift from faith to disbelief, therefore making you believe that the word spoken, read or heard is untrue. However, the enemy can deceive the word out of your heart is how he is going to triumph and be successful. BUT AGAIN, THE DEVIL IS A LIAR! See, the reason why the enemy is familiar with the heart is because Sin entered the world through Lucifer's heart (**Isaiah 14:12 and Ezekiel 28:15).**

It is a known fact that sin is the enjoyable resting place in the heart since its inception date with the devil.

Prayer agents, we have one heart given by God which puts a standard and command on us that we belong to Him. With that understanding we pray the word of God. It then stirs up our faith and we keep it there because our heart needs to match the heart of God.

Building a Relationship with God in Communication

Presence, by definition, is "the state or fact of existing, occurring, or being present in a place or thing; a person or thing that exists or is present in a place but is not seen."

The presence of a place or a thing can be distracted or disrupted by anyone that is allowed to be a part of the connected experience. Let us go deeper, when you are in the presence of someone or something, an atmosphere is either created, established, or shifted. Have you ever entered a room, or an environment and you felt a change? The people in the room may have been engaging in a discreet conversation prior to your entrance and when you entered the room the conversation ended. A few things may have happened:

1. The conversation could have possibly been about you
2. The conversation could have possibly been about someone else
3. The conversation could have possibly been discussed at the inappropriate time

There could be many explanations to support the change in the room, but one thing is for sure, your presence made a difference. The atmosphere shifted when your presence showed up. The people in the room respected your presence in so many words because their behaviors changed.

Presence can establish an atmosphere. I say that because presence causes an impact in the environment and the atmosphere by the spirit that is released. Thereby causing the space or environment to be submissive to the time, reason, and season of the released spirit.

Presence can create an atmosphere causing whatever the occupied space was before to align with the authoritative spirit. Whew, that is deep! When the presence shows up, there is enough dominant power on the inside to cause creation to happen where something is already in operation.

Getting God's attention does not mean that you are literally going to His face, and into the heavens to pray. The way you get His attention is by getting into His presence. Psalms 100:4 gives us guidance on how to execute this experience.

Enter into his gates with thanksgiving, and into his courts with praise be thankful unto him and bless his name.

- Psalms 100:4

The word that blesses me from this scripture is enter. We find our way to where God's presence is, and we enter in, thanking Him, going further into praising Him, then we thank Him some more, and praise Him even the more. I want you to understand that the place of God's presence is not limited to a physical locale, geographical or territorial area. Wherever you summon, seek or beckon for His presence to be, is where it appears. Once you are in the presence of God and you have His attention, you can then feel, hear, see, smell, and know His response is around you. There is a calming feeling that overtakes every part of your body and you feel like you are in a safe place. The presence of God is the place where dreams come true, visions are released, and communication is established. The Lord begins to share with you HIS heart, HIS will, HIS thoughts concerning you. The more you visit the deeper the conversation becomes. You begin to learn how God enjoys the dialogue between you Him. From there, you receive His response back to you in various ways. I am telling you, when you begin to build relationship with God in communication, there is nothing the enemy can say or do that will cause you to doubt His word.

Meditate on these Scriptures:

Jeremiah 29:12-14 AMP

Then you will call on me and come and pray to me, and I will listen to you.[13] You will seek me and find me when you seek me with all your heart. I will be found by you," declares the Lord, "and will bring you back from captivity.[b]

Psalms 16:11 AMP

You make known to me the path of life; you will fill me with joy in your presence, with eternal pleasures at your right hand.

Revelations 21:3-5 KJV

And I heard a great voice out of heaven saying, Behold, the tabernacle of God is with men, and he will dwell with them, and they shall be his people, and God himself shall be with them, and be their God. And God shall wipe away all tears from their eyes; and there shall be no more death, neither sorrow, nor crying, neither shall there be any more pain: for the former things are passed away. And he that sat upon the throne said, Behold, I make all things new.

When you want the attention of someone, you will do what is required to attract and captivate them to the point where it will yield a response.

I want to look at two encounters in the word of God where entering the presence of God caused exchanged dialogue and when God answers request from being in his presence.

Physical Presence of God

MARK 5:25-34 KJV

And a certain woman, which had an issue of blood twelve years,

26 And had suffered many things of many physicians, and had spent all that she had, and was nothing bettered, but rather grew worse,

27 When she had heard of Jesus, came in the press behind, and touched his garment.

28 For she said, If I may touch but his clothes, I shall be whole.

29 And straightway the fountain of her blood was dried up; and she felt in her body that she was healed of that plague.

30 And Jesus, immediately knowing in himself that virtue had gone out of him, turned him about in the press, and said, Who touched my clothes?

31 And his disciples said unto him, Thou seest the multitude thronging thee, and sayest thou, Who touched me?

32 And he looked round about to see her that had done this thing.

33 But the woman fearing and trembling, knowing what was done in her, came and fell before him, and told him all the truth.

34 And he said unto her, Daughter, thy faith hath made thee whole; go in peace and be whole of thy plague.

Here we find a certain woman who had an issue for twelve years. This same woman entered the presence of medical professionals seeking counsel with no result. When the woman heard of Jesus, she then followed along with the multitude, (entering His presence) but she did not stop there. Being a part of the multitude following Jesus was not good enough for her because she was dealing with an issue that just settling for His presence was not sufficient.

The woman pressed through the multitude in pursuit of getting to Jesus because she felt if she could touch something on Him even if it's the hem of his garment, by faith she would be made whole of her issue.

As you continue to read the story, Jesus turned into the crowd asking, "Who touched me?" and saw her still there. There became an exchange of dialogue as the woman begin to share with Jesus why she touched him, and he said back to her, "Thy faith hath made thee whole; go in peace, and be whole of thy plague." HALLELUJAH! What a great example of what being in the presence of God is all about. We desire more of Him, and we receive it based upon our faith.

Can I point one more thing out from this scripture? The healing of the woman was complete as a result of her staying in His presence long enough for her to see Him face-to-face, confess to Him her issue, and receive His permissible authority to depart from his presence. Isn't that something?

Here is the second example of building relationship with God in communication regarding Hannah in I Samuel chapter 1.

The story of Hannah is yet another great example of building relationship with God in communication (prayer). Here we find a woman, married to a priest but unable to conceive a child because the Lord shut her womb. This is something the Lord purposely caused to happen as He knew that a miracle would come forth as a result. Hannah did not pray for her marriage, for money, or even other spiritual gifts; it was her desire that God would grant her mercy on the very thing *"HE"* placed on her life.

The faith of Hannah was fearless, ambitious, and hopeful as it came out of brokenness, disappointment, rejection and abandonment. The more she sought the Lord, the stronger her faith increased. As she entered His presence, the Bible does not record God ever speaking back to her audibly or releasing a word of promise that what she was praying for would come to pass. During the conversation with her husband, the priest, and sharing how she wanted God to give her this miracle, the priest agreed in prayer with her and said "May the God of Israel grant you what you have asked of Him". (**I Samuel 1:17 KJV**) Interesting! I am inclined to believe the reason the priest, Elkanah said these words to her was by way of the spirit of God. From a place of authority, the husband is the priest of the house so whatever blessing he pronounces over his family, God honors.

The Lord hears the prayers of His men. It seems to me that when Elkanah came into agreement with his wife concerning the prayers she offered unto the Lord, that God responded.

As the chapter goes forward, you will see that the Lord did JUST THAT! He opened her womb, planted a seed and then came Samuel. What was so amazing is that she was specific in her request to God in prayer for what she wanted, and the Lord closed her womb so she can pray for what HE wanted. She desired a man-child and the Lord had a prophet in heaven that was needed to be released in the earth. Here is what I would call a *Win, win* situation that could have only been discovered and manifested by relationship and communication between God and a willing vessel. Communication is the vehicle that builds trust between God and his people. It causes HIS "will to be done on earth as it is in heaven." **Matthew 6:10**

January 2019, I had an experience with God in prayer. I had been agitated in my emotions and did not have an understanding as to why I was feeling that way. I felt like my emotions were out of control and felt a little hopeless. As the evening hours approached, I decided to have an encounter with the Lord. I listened to the "Diary of Juanita Bynum" CD project and began to cry uncontrollably on the floor. As I was crying and weeping, I still did not have a reason as to why I was in this state but just felt like I needed to get some things out. I must admit, it felt good to cleanse my soul, my heart, my mind from the aggravation of emotions I had been carrying throughout the day.

The Lord led me to read chapter 4 of Colossians. Still remaining in his presence, I heard Him say to me again to read verse 12 of chapter 4 in the New Living Translation (NLT). Before going there, I heard God say, "I'm fixing your heart. I am touching your heart from hatred and anger. I am healing you. I'm with you and you can flow in my will when your heart is delivered." I cried and screamed on the floor. As I proceeded to the Bible, I was hesitant because I questioned, "Lord, what if I'm making this scripture up?" After exploring this thought and moving forward with reading the scripture I was led to, here is what I found.
Colossians 4:12 NLT

"Epaphras, a member of your own fellowship and a servant of Christ Jesus, sends you his greetings. He always prays earnestly for you, asking God to make you strong and perfect, fully confident that you are following the whole will of God."

After reading that scripture, I just remember saying so loudly, "**GOD YOU HEARD MY PRAYERS, AND, LORD, I HEARD YOU SPEAK TO ME.**" It was a moment where I was so thankful that my relationship with the Father is so authentic that He would speak to me in my time of need. I was hesitant to read the scripture but look at what was there for me. I needed strength, I needed confidence and to be able to follow the whole Will of God. For me to do so, my heart had to be healed. Only by relationship in communication with God, could I have come to this understanding.

Transparent moment: As a Christian believer, you will always discover that building relationship with God is an ongoing process. When you think you have him figured out because you have been "walking with Him" so long, then you will see there is much more to Him than you can imagine. I do not know about you but there are times where I have found myself breaking up with God repeatedly. It seems as if life gets so strenuous, overwhelming, and breaks you to a point where you are just DONE! God you can keep all of this you may say. Has anyone been there before? I recall going through one of the toughest periods of my life where I felt as if I could not pray, praise, worship, or read the word. Anything that was spiritually connected, I felt I was not a part of. Seemed as if my circumstance won me over and that my breakup with God happened and He left me.

Can you relate to that?
What was your "separation" experience?

_____

_____

_____

_____

_____

_____

_____

_____

_____

_____

_____

I found myself going days, weeks, and even months where I was doing life on my own. Waking up angry, bitter, negative, complaining, just over life itself. But one thing, I have come to know in this life, is that when you ease up off of God, He has a way of easing up off of you but still close to you where He will not allow you to fall. God is a gentleman and is never going to force himself on you. He is so gracious that he gives us the freedom of choice. With this freedom of choice, it is full of the patience, grace, mercy and compassion of God. It is like God knows where you are, and fully aware of what you are engaging in but will wait patiently on the appointed time for you to recover and return back to him. THANK YOU, JESUS.

After a while, you get tired of being angry. It becomes exhausting. One day, I said to myself, "Jackie, the only way out of this is for you to go away and isolate yourself with God." I took three days away from everyone to a resort just to be with God. I made sure that I did not take my best clothes, but just my tallit, my white prayer sheet, my Bible, and a journal. Each day during my time away, I put my phone on do not disturb. I did not have an agenda, focus, strategy or any of that. I went to God broken, vulnerable and all I was expecting was for Him to restore me. Every morning when I woke up and every night before bed, all I could do was cry until I was exhausted from crying. God allowed me to bring my pain and my brokenness to Him and He embraced me as I let it all out. He did not speak to me right away, but just let me weep. As each new day approached, so did He. He softly spoke to me and I wrote everything down in my journal. By the last and final day, the Lord sent me outside of the resort and had me stare at a waterfall as I stood under a tree. He spoke to me about my identity, the season I was in and the season I was getting ready to enter.

He restored my soul, my mind, my heart and put me in a place where I could trust in Him again.

What are you saying Jackie? I am saying when you are feeling numb to the spirit, or at times angry with God (because we all have been there) all He wants is confession, isolation, and vulnerability. God listens to us in our times of weakness. As a matter of fact, the Bible says His strength is made perfect in our times of weakness. I want to share some of what the Lord gave me at my point of restoration.

God said, "I had to harden you up, so that you can know what it feels like to deal with hard things."

He then said to me, "I didn't allow Elijah's ministry to end under the juniper tree or in a cave, but I brought him out and carried him to the completion of his assignment."

WOW! THANK YOU, LORD! With this revelation from the Lord concerning the prophet Elijah in I Kings chapter 19, I found myself aligning with the emotion he experienced. Elijah was sitting under the juniper tree depressed and asked God to take his life. Jezebel was out to kill him and the only thing he was doing was releasing the word of God. Elijah was fulfilling the work of the Lord. He ended up in a cave and the Lord spoke to him in that cave (I Kings 19:9-18), asking Elijah the question "What are you doing in here"? The Lord had ministry for him to fulfill by way of anointing three men, one of which was Elisha his successor.

The ministry of Elisha and him receiving the mantle of Elijah would not have occurred if the Lord would not have spoken to him and Elijah obeyed. In so many words, the Lord was telling me to *"COME FROM UNDER THE JUNIPER TREE AND OUT OF THE CAVE"*

See, these are words that the Lord says when you step away from the noise and find a quiet place with Him. Being a prayer agent is not glamourous.
It is not lights, camera, and action! But there are times where you will be faced with challenges that can cause you to doubt yourself. STAY WITH GOD! Find your isolated place with God and know that you are yet building relationship with Him. As a matter of fact, each challenge, hurdle, circumstance you face makes your relationship with Him EVEN stronger!

Prayer Agents by Jackie A. Jones Jr.

PART II

Prayer Strategies

Oxford dictionary defines the word *strategy* as "a plan of action designed to achieve a long-term or overall aim." In other words, a strategy causes a person to draw a blueprint outlining the details on where and how to build the best foundation for a successful outcome. In the world there are various avenues of communication: telephone, video chat, social media and email just to name a few.

Each of these channels give us the ability to communicate with family, friends, co-workers, or whomever our intended audience may be at that time. The difference between all of them is their strategy. The strategy used for video chat is for the person to see and hear, email is used to send and receive files by typing messages, and social media is used to network and connect with a broader audience all over the world. The telephone's function is for one to hear and to speak. Mobile devices such as cell phones, iPads and tablets, provides the flexibility to choose how you want to communicate with various avenues to choose from. They provide you with the ability to execute such functions like video chat, text, email, and download. However, it is up to the individual on what option is best suited for their need. Whatever function of operation is chosen be it the device or media outlet, it's going to always be what it was created to be and that is a communication tool. In prayer, we have access to seek God for immeasurable and unlimited things. Meaning, you have the freedom to create in prayer the strategy to reach your intended target. For example, if freedom from financial debt is what you are requesting, the first thing to do is set a strategy in the natural on ways to accomplish that goal. Such goals would include a savings plan, investment options, credit repair, paying bills on time and so forth.

The Bible says in **I Corinthians 15:46 KJV**
"However, the spiritual [the immortal life] is not first, but the physical [the mortal life]; then the spiritual.

Create a realistic plan of strategy in the natural that will hold you accountable in seeking results you desire to see. For example, if I am believing God for exponential growth in my business, it is my responsibility to identify the specific areas that I want to see grow. The next step would be to write the vision or budget plan and put a timeline together that will set me up for success and track my progress. Once the plan has been put in place, then search the word of God locating scriptures on increase, spend a consecutive time of choice meditating on those scriptures, set a time frame within those seven days to pray daily and speak faith confessions.

The strategy provides divine direction and causes you to pray in direct symmetry to the place you are going. Makes sense?

Take a moment to write down a strategy you are currently working or need to work on:

_____

_____

_____

_____

_____

_____

_____

_____

_____

<u>Praying the word of God</u>

The purpose of praying the word of God is for us to remind God of his word. Prayer agents are kingdom administrators, receptionists, and calendar managers. Which means we document, schedule, and keep God informed of every promise He made to His people in His word. In prayer, you need a direct symmetry, a line, a target and the support of heaven backing you up, as this is necessary for God to manifest. The word of God is the WILL of God. As mentioned in **Isaiah 55:11 KJV:** "as the word goes out of your mouth it shall not return back void;" therefore, as we send out the word of God, we are promised to get results.

Praying the word of God avoids repetitious wording and advances us from remaining on a lower surface level of prayer. The word shifts us into a deeper place in God as we begin to talk His language, His heart and His will. The word of God, according to **Hebrews 4:12 says** "For the word of God is quick, and powerful, and sharper than any two-edged sword, piercing even to the dividing asunder of soul and spirit, and of the joints and marrow, and is a discerner of the thoughts and intents of the heart."

Sounds violent, destructive, and painful, yet informative and powerful as it pertains to its purpose. The purpose of the word of God based upon Hebrews 4:12 is to be quick, release power, divide, and provide knowledge and insight. Yes Lord! Words have power, therefore the words you release employ your angels to fulfill the assignment you give them to do. **Psalms 103:20** mentions how the "angels excel in strength at the mention of God's word." When you pray, the word of God comes alive in your prayer language with authority and faith. The authority lies in your voice to decree and declare that the word of God is law in the heavens and in the earth.

Therefore, faith is ignited within you as you believe in the word you are releasing in prayer.

The angels now have a directional focus on where to go and what to do. Some believers may find it very challenging to pray the word of God due to the content and lack of obtaining revelation in reading the word. The Bible, as mentioned in the introductory section of the book, can be perceived as intimidating to a great number of new believers and those who have been on their Christian walk for a long time.

Especially if they are not sure on how to pronounce names of bible characters or finding connection with bible stories and modern-day life. A new believer may find it challenging to connect with the word if they have only been taught one translation such as King James Version.

I remember as a child being given the handheld size King James Bible. It had a bright orange leather cover and it was the New Testament version only. I recall thinking to myself, "wow, this bible is small, and this is all I have to read?" My mother had this massive bible placed on a glass table with photos on the inside of it. The bible she had was more captivating because I saw visuals of characters and the writing seemed easier to read. The difference between my mother's bible and my bible was that she had the entire 66 books and it was larger in size. However, the bible I had was a limited read.

My teenage years, I remember this black leather bible my mother carried around with her to church. This bible was filled with colorful highlights, handwritten messages on the pages, and the leather cover on the bible was wearing out from being transported from place to place. There was a time in my earlier years of school where I experienced bullying from a few of my peers.

I was home from school due to a slip disk which prevented me from being able to walk normally. In my mind, I was relieved that there was a physical ailment occurring in my life so that I could "prevent" dealing with these bullies. As I was home alone, parents were at work, I grabbed my mother's bible and opened it up. It was the King James Version bible and I did not understand anything I was reading. The curiosity of my mom finding knowledge in this book caused me to find out myself what is this about. Yes, I was raised in the church and believed in God, but I did not open a bible as a younger kid or even in my early teenage years. What I learned about the word of God, came from my mother, sunshine band and purity class from church, and watching preachers on television. By the way, watching church on tv was my "guilty pleasure" as a kid and a teenager. The day I picked up this bible, I went to the book of Psalms and I remember saying "Lord, talk to me from this book". Kid you not, there was a number of Psalms I read, and it was so specific to my need that it sounded as if the words was something that I wrote down. The scripture dealt with having God to deal with my enemies and to silence them who speak against me.

The words came to life right before my eyes in a translation that I did not understand. I recall crying my eyes out and, in a vision, seeing those bullies from my school. It was like I could see myself saying these words and resolution was coming to me from God. The spirit of the Lord spoke to me and said, I am going to heal your back from this pain. Mind you, I have not been able to walk normally because of the pain from this affliction, but I placed my hand on my back, and I stood up. As I stood up, the pain was gone completely.

When I returned to school the next day, there was a confidence on the inside of me and I knew God handled my enemies. True story, those bullies that were tormenting me, were silenced. There was nothing I had to say or do when I got to school. The Lord handled it someway, somehow.

The moral of my sharing of this story is, if you put the word in you, revelation will come. God wants your willingness and vulnerability to engage in His word and He will do the rest. There are numerous amounts of biblical translations to choose from: Amplified, New Living Translation, Good News Bible, New English Standard just to name a few. Growing up, I was only exposed to King James Version therefore the only way that I could seek to understand was by way of revelation.

The word of God is very much alive and relevant to everyday life. The word can be made relatively easy to connect with if you ask God in prayer to give you divine understanding.

Proverbs Chapter 4:7-wisdom is the principal thing therefore get wisdom and with all thy getting get understanding. If you pray for wisdom when you open the word of God, out of your obedience he will answer. **James 1:5 (MSG)** says: "If you don't know what you're doing, pray to the Father. He loves to help. You'll get his help and won't be condescended to when you ask for it."

For new believers and those who lost their zeal for seeking the Lord in prayer, I would encourage reading the book of Psalms as a starting point. Psalms express variations of emotions ranging from questions being asked to God, transparency, praise, worship, singing, prayers and more. If you pray a Psalm during your prayer time on a consistent basis, you will begin to familiarize yourself with the word.
Therefore, you release the glory of God, increase your faith, and create an atmosphere that causes God to respond to your request.

Let's read the commonly used Psalms 23 for example;

Psalm 23 King James Version (KJV)

The Lord is my shepherd; I shall not want.

2 He maketh me to lie down in green pastures: he leadeth me beside the still waters.

3 He restoreth my soul: he leadeth me in the paths of righteousness for his name's sake.

4 Yea, though I walk through the valley of the shadow of death, I will fear no evil: for thou art with me; thy rod and thy staff they comfort me.

5 Thou preparest a table before me in the presence of mine enemies: thou anointest my head with oil; my cup runneth over.

6 Surely goodness and mercy shall follow me all the days of my life: and I will dwell in the house of the Lord forever.

Praying the word of God can be done in various ways. Here are a few methods I recommend:

- Pray the scripture(s) verbatim,
- Extract from the scripture what is vital for the prayer focus/target (ex: certain phrases, or wording from that scripture).
- Combine verses throughout the entire Bible tailored to the need of the prayer.

Let us explore a few prayer examples utilizing Psalms 23 with the recommended methods previously mentioned.

Example #1-Specific Scripture(s)

Father, in the name of Jesus, I thank you and praise you for are **my shepherd.** You oh Lord are the one who covers me, provides for me, takes care of me in all areas therefore **I shall not want** anything. I find all I need in you God for you complete me. Thank you for **making me to lie down in green pastures,** causing me to be fruitful, successful, and be at peace. **You lead me beside the still waters** which allows me oh God to be in a place of security. Though the waters are moving, and waves can be tossed to and fro, **I will not fear because thou art with me.** I thank you God for being the **restorer of my soul and leading me in righteous paths for your name's sake.** Every path I walk in God is ordered by you. Every path leads me to a favorable place in you. **Yea, though I walk through the valley of the shadow of death, I will not fear for you God are with me** through it all. **Thy rod and thy staff they comfort me,** providing me the assurance that I am under your guidance. As the shepherd, you will not allow anything to happen to me, but you stick beside me. Lord, for every enemy that seeks after my soul to destroy my life, **you prepare a table before me in their presence.** In that same place, you **anoint my head with oil,** and release the blessing of overflow to happen right in the face of my enemies so they can see my **cup running over** continually. I have this assurance now Lord, that **goodness and mercy shall follow me all the days of my life, and I will dwell, reside, take rest in the house of the Lord forever.** In Jesus name, Amen

Example #2-Extract from the Scriptures (Prayer of protection-Psalms 23)

Father in the name of Jesus, I call on you to be my protector who keeps guard and watch over my soul. God, I give you praise for being all I need and because I am confident in who you are, I shall never be in a place that I am without. Father, you are with me during the times I experience valley moments where I feel as if I am about to lose it, give it all up, and my life is over. Yet I praise you now at this time and season of my life because in the midst of how I feel in the valley I will not fear because I know you are with me. You being with me God lets me know that I am protected from death and the hand of every enemy. I dwell in your spirit, your word, your house that covers me and gives me restoration in my soul. I thank you Father! In Jesus Name.

Example #3-Combining Scriptures throughout the Bible (Prayer of Confidence)

Father you are the great and mighty God who sits upon the circle of the earth and looks over your people. You are the God who provides your heart, and your spirit to your people and makes ways out of no way. Father you specialize in the impossible, and you cause us to have faith in you through everything we go through. For this we have a confidence that you began a good work in us. The work you have done and are still doing gives us spiritual understanding, provides strength to us in the power of your might, and a dwelling place where we can remain in you. Lord, thank you for anointing our heads with the oil so that we can confidently align our minds with the mind of you, will of you, thoughts of you as we seek to bring your kingdom in the earth as it is in heaven. Praise you Father God, for you cause us to triumph over our enemies just as you did when you died on the cross. Your name be glorified, edified and forever released in this earth. We speak in confidence and authority because your word says that in you we live, we move, and we have our being. We are seated in heavenly places with you Father, therefore we are established in royalty, commanding all powers under us to submit to the anointing of God on our lives. We give you praise now, IN JESUS NAME, AMEN

These three examples are just my thoughts, but please feel free to find your connection to the word of God. What I love about God's word is that it is so prophetic and full of revelation!
A person can read a passage of scripture like Psalms 23, 365 days, or for 30 years and will find a new revelation better than the last time. The written word of God is just like God himself, meaning it is always speaking cause our God is always speaking. The Lord designed His word to be that way for his people so that we are always searching, seeking, desiring more of Him every time we read. Prayer agents should always be hungry and thirsty for the word of God. Always having an open ear and applying new word in a new way in prayer.

Connecting to the word of God must become your daily appetite and routine just as we have both in the natural. For example, our daily routine includes shower, dress, brush our teeth, drink liquids, think with our brains to accomplish various tasks, and more. Everything we do daily has a reaction to it. Brushing your teeth produces fresh breath. Taking a shower produces a clean body with a fresh scent. Dressing yourself gives a fresh new look, drinking water (liquids) gives hydration and new energy. Just as these routines cause reactions, so does the word of God when applied to our lives daily.

The result of learning His word causes us to receive fresh revelation, fresh word, fresh oil, fresh anointing, fresh hearing, fresh sight, and more. WHEW! Thank you, Jesus!

Prayer Beyond Emotions

Jesus during His time of ministry was 100% God and 100% man at the same time yet He did not sin. Jesus understands how it feels to be tempted and what it feels like to be emotional.

Jesus cried when His best friend Lazarus died (*natural*)- John 11:30-36

Yet, with authority He caused Lazarus to live (*spiritual*)- John 11:38-44

Jesus was tempted by Satan on his fast (*natural*) Matthew 4:1-2

Yet, He rebukes him (*spiritual*)-Matthew 4:3-11

Jesus, considered not fulfilling the Will of God (*natural*) Luke 22:42-44

Yet, he prayed for the WILL of God to be performed (*spiritual*)

Jesus was angry by clearing out the temple (*natural*) Matthew 21:12-13

Yet, He established order and operated in the spirit of healing (*spiritual*) Matthew 21:14

As we look at some of the experiences Jesus encountered during his time on earth, we can align ourselves with some or maybe all these situations. Jesus provides us with some of the greatest responses in these scriptures listed above. When you lose a loved one, it is okay to grieve, cry, experience sadness but you can speak to that situation and cause life to occur. Now, it may not be God's will for the deceased loved one to come back to life, but you can speak to the emotional areas of grief and put an expiration date on them. In times of temptation when you are the most focused on your dreams, goals, new journey of life, here comes the past lurking around you to lure you out of focus. Jesus quoted the word of God every time by saying "IT IS WRITTEN." The Bible says in **1 Corinthians 10:13 AMP 13** that No temptation [regardless of its source] has overtaken or enticed you that is not common to human experience [nor is any temptation unusual or beyond human resistance].

God is a God of order. Everything that was made in this world was done intentionally and strategically with the mind of God. Even Jesus coming into the earth to fulfill ministry was done intentionally in the will of the Father. As He walked the earth to explore the things God has made, He had an expectation for the people in the earth to manage and maintain what was created. For example, sheep was placed in the care of shepherds to protect, guide, clean and more. The temple was created for the Father in heaven to bring forth prayer, worship, praise, and the word of God. There were other uses for the temple during the time when Jesus was on earth, but the focus was for the kingdom of God. However, we find in **Matthew 21:12-14 KJV** where Jesus saw that the temple was operating in a different manner.

¹² And Jesus went into the temple of God, and cast out all them that sold and bought in the temple, and overthrew the tables of the moneychangers, and the seats of them that sold doves,

¹³ And said unto them, It is written, My house shall be called the house of prayer; but ye have made it a den of thieves.¹⁴ And the blind and the lame came to him in the temple; and he healed them.

Jesus is looking at the temple being out of order and saying to the people that this place is called the house of prayer. Meaning this is the place where prayer is offered unto God continually. The environment, culture and atmosphere of the temple should resemble nothing but prayer. As you can see from this experience, that having a place of prayer is vital to God. When the people in the temple shifted the focus from prayer to a marketplace, it became a huge problem. It caused the people to enter the temple with a different mindset that deviated from seeking God, to focusing on other things. Jesus gave a great demonstration of what was happening in the spirit by him doing something that may have been drastic to some. He turned over the tables, shifted the room to focus on Him, and said to them what this temple is supposed to be and what they have turned it into. That moment was so priceless as it created a physical view of how it looked in the spirit and that was disarray. Could you imagine the look on everyone is faces in the temple when Jesus turned the tables over? He interrupted what was beginning to become common and reestablished the order in the house.

The best part of this is the last line of this particular passage of scripture that goes from Jesus saying what the temple should be to healing the blind and the lame who entered the temple. Wow! Jesus showed them what this place should encounter by way of prayer and that is miracles, signs and wonders.

There was a time when I was in school and one of my peers was very controlling to quite a few people. This person was very cunning with words, intimidating and would be very judgmental and condescending to students in the school. During the school year, I would find myself coming home going straight into my room where I would remain there for hours.

Unlike most children who would go outside riding bikes, playing with other kids on the block, I would be in my room praying. There were times in school during this particular year, where I was overwhelmed by this individual. Therefore, when I came home, I needed to let out my tension or anxiety from the day and words spoken to me. There was this one day where I had enough. When I got home, I went into my room, locked the door and I cried out to God like something serious. The Lord showed me this vision of a throne adorned with white linen and I saw angel like images.

It was as if it was the most beautiful place in the world. There was something beaconing me to come towards it and all I felt was comfort and safety. In that place, I laid down and wept and I heard this voice saying to me *"all is well."* I realized I was laying on my bed in the natural the same way I was laying there in my vision which was on my face. As I got up to gather myself, I begin to go into war on behalf of my spirit and attack the spirit of my peer. As I prayed, I told the Lord to show this person the error of their ways and to not make it easy for them in this season. I begin to bind up the spirit and sent the angels on assignment to handle this person. Although, I was not very versed in scriptures to use in prayer I still prayed because I knew God could interpret what I was trying to convey.

As I went back to school, I noticed this student had not been in attendance for a few days which was odd cause they rarely missed school. It was then brought to my attention that the family of my peer abruptly moved out of state which means a transfer occurred. Let me tell you something, I could do nothing but laugh. I knew within myself that this was a result of my prayer. Who would have thought that God would hear the prayer of a teenage boy who did not quote scriptures in prayer or even use fancy words, but it reached him! I LOVE THE LORD! God answered me according to the sentiment of my heart.

Instead of physically attacking this individual, I went to God in the spirit to learn how to attack.

I knew then that prayer is my weapon of defense against the enemy.

The testimony from this experience happened when this student returned to the school after being gone for an extensive period of time and apologized to me for the wrongdoing, they caused me over the years. WOW! Did you hear what I said? I was given an apology and we became good friends from that moment on. God is so faithful to his people. "What I do by faith, Favor will back me up". I am telling you the truth.

Life can throw curve balls, offer teachable lessons, and place you in challenging circumstances. The pressures of life can bring challenges that are assigned to "knock you off your square". However, those same things are used as vehicles for prayer as life experiences push us to pray. Without seeing, hearing, obtaining knowledge of the challenge, and having challenging experiences, there would not be anything to seek the Lord for. It is okay for us to enter prayer while experiencing personal problems and emotional circumstances.

We as the body of Christ encounter problems for the purpose of triggering the posture and position of prayer.

It is vital to seek understanding concerning the Will of God for your life, which can only be found in the word and by prayer. The lack of understanding God's will can make you feel life is too much to handle. It can also make you feel at times like giving up. During those moments where you may feel hopeless and purposeless, is when something on the inside of you encourages you to keep going. Praying the WILL of God to be performed in your life (Matthew 6:10 Thy Kingdom, come thy WILL BE done in earth as it is in heaven) will strengthen you.

We as believers can be supported during our walk with God in knowing that he understands us. God knows everything we feel in our emotions as Hebrews 4:15 For we do not have a High Priest who is unable to sympathize and understand our weaknesses and temptations, but One who has been tempted [knowing exactly how it feels to be human] in every respect as we are, yet without [committing any] sin.

I love this scripture because it reassures me that God is truly with me. He empathizes with me when I am experiencing trials, tribulations and when I cannot express what I feel, He knows already. You know how you share a feeling on the inside with a person and you hear the words *"I understand?"* There are times when someone would say those words to me, and I respond back like *"do you really"?* The response is not to diminish them, but we all have a set of emotions and it is actually not a truthful statement when another person says they understand. Reason being is because we may have gone through the same type of trial, experience the same type of loss, may have even seen the same problems. However, there is a difference in one person who endures verses the other. Unless you are literally on the inside of my body feeling the exact same emotion, then you cannot "understand" how I feel. Oh, but Jesus who created me, knows how many hairs are on my head knows EVERYTHING concerning me. When this scripture says He understands our weakness and temptation, of course He knows because He created it all. Makes sense? Jesus became flesh and dwelt among us to feel what we feel and endure what we endure. My God! Thank you, Lord!

When we pray, we are to be charged to enter the spirit of God where confidence, authority and boldness lies. The bible says in Hebrews 4:16 Therefore let us [with privilege] approach the throne of grace [that is, the throne of God's gracious favor] with confidence and without fear, so that we may receive mercy [for our failures] and find [His amazing] grace to help in time of need [an appropriate blessing, coming just at the right moment].

I prophecy to those reading this book right now, that you will have a new zeal, new passion, new lens and scope for reading the word of the Lord. I command you to be OPEN NOW IN JESUS NAME, to be a recipient of fresh things. HALLELUJAH! BE OPEN TO HEAR, SEE, SMELL, TASTE, AND EVEN TOUCH what the Lord has to say to His people. I pray activation in all spiritual gifts and that when you pray the word of God, things will be established, and HIS LIGHT will SHINE UPON YOUR WAYS IN JESUS NAME. GO FORTH IN THE WORD, WRESTLE WITH THE WORD, SPEAK THE WORD, DECLARE AND DECREE LAWS WITH THE WORD! May you have legislative authority with the word of the Lord. Come forth, take over the world with the word of God.

Intentional Prayer Time with God

The word intentional simply means "done on purpose; deliberate." To be intentional is not being forced, grudging, or resistant but it is a willingness to accomplish a thing. Intentional behavior or initiatives are activated when a prayer agent says, "I see the need, I understand the purpose, now let me find a way to make it happen." With intent of receiving results, the prayer agent asks questions like:

- "What does it take for_____ to manifest?
- What is in the mind of God concerning the earth, the church, my life?
- Lord, you gave me this to pray for, so how can I be the midwife to pray this through?"

This place then becomes a compelling force into God's presence where you do not wait on Him or wait on anyone else, but you go after Him for yourself.

Isaiah 55:6,8-9 KJV

Seek ye the Lord while he may be found, call ye upon him while he is near: For my thoughts are not your thoughts, neither are your ways my ways, saith the Lord. For as the heavens are higher than the earth, so are my ways higher than your ways, and my thoughts than your thoughts.

Prayer Experience

The Lord placed me in a season where I had to wake up on Sunday mornings during the 5am hour, worship Him, read His word and seek Him on behalf of local ministries all over the world. During that time, He would speak to me concerning what will happen for the day and would reveal what to pray and intercede for. **Psalms 63:1-2** describes the cry of my heart toward God during that time:

O God, thou art my God; early will I seek thee: my soul thirsteth for thee, my flesh longeth for thee in a dry and thirsty land, where no water is; To see thy power and thy glory, so as I have seen thee in the sanctuary.

One Sunday, the Lord led to me pray for people all over the world who experienced childhood trauma by way of abuse. My heart grieved for people who experienced physical, verbal, mental, and sexual abuse and have not healed from the memory of it. As I began to cry out, I was led to pray for those who would attend worship services on that Sunday all over the world, who suffer in silence, that they would be healed, delivered, and restored. When I arrived at church, in conversation with a few individuals that day, I encountered some individuals who freely opened up and shared with me the horrors of their childhood trauma. My mouth dropped open and I was in AWE that I prayed for that on that morning. The Lord brought freedom to them and he had them to converse directly with me to show that the prayers offered were in order. WOW!

I admonish prayer agents to set aside private prayer time for your local ministry whether it is the day before Sunday service or the day of.

The Lord is always speaking, and it is for us to intercede (interrupt) what the enemy desires to attack during our fellowship time of worship on Sunday or whatever days are set aside for our service(s).

When you pray, you are having conversation with the Lord. You are speaking to Him and in return He begins to share His will with you. The Lord is always speaking so He begins to share what He wants to say. Sometimes it is about you, and other times it is about Him or the world. What happens is, He gives you information for you to regurgitate it back to Him with His word on it.
It's like conversation with anyone: you repeat back what you hear to affirm the individual that you are listening, and you assure them that you are there to support what you heard. The affirmation and assurance present an offering of help to the individual you are in conversation with.

Prayer allows God to be vulnerable, revealing His mysteries to you for you to do something about them that ultimately pushes Him to release and manifest. God cannot be on earth in His truest form. If that happens, the world is over. We cannot see Him or take all of Him in His rare form. Therefore, God needs a conduit, a vessel and a vehicle to use that will hear Him and allow Him to use them to get the information from heaven to earth. This comes with maturity in prayer. The more time you spend with God, the more He opens up to you and reveal. The more immature you are with God, the more your relationship with Him becomes about you. The focus is directed toward you, on you, about you, for you and begins growing to the point where it is never about Him and what He wants done. We as prayer agents, should desire His Will for our lives, the world, the nation and the earth at all times.

At the beginning of each new year, my church has 21 days of prayer and fasting. The vision of my Archbishop some years ago was for the entire congregation, and those who wanted to connect with us outside of our membership, to fast and attend one hour of prayer service each day. The beginning of the year was the "intentional" time we devoted ourselves to seeking the Lord for vision concerning our year both as a church and in our personal lives. January 2019, it was my desire to not only align with the church but for my own personal time with the Lord. I tried every day during this time to spend one hour of personal prayer at minimum with the Lord. As we got closer to our 21st day, I begin to increase my time with the Lord from one hour to 90 minutes, to two hours of straight prayer. There were days where I would pray for one straight hour and spend the next hour in quiet meditation. The experience was not about just challenging myself to spend "time" with God, but also for me to go deeper with my approach in prayer. It was my desire for me during those 21 days, to experience God in a new way as I wanted to know the height, length, width and depth of prayer just as the Bible says in **Ephesians 3:18-20.** We will explore more about prayer agendas and assignments a little later in this section.

I recall attending prayer service each night with a new oil, anointing, and fresh revelation, and I would hear from those who would attend say to me, "Elder Jackie, there is something different about you." My countenance began to change, the way prayer was delivered and how intercession was offered was like nothing I had ever experienced before. Spending intentional time in prayer causes you to define your voice pattern in prayer, receive downloads from heaven, increases stamina and endurance with the Lord, hearing of his voice more clearly, and retaining the word of God. There were times in prayer where I was unfamiliar with certain scriptures or even unsure where they were located but things would come to me like "strengthened with all might" as I prayed. I've heard that before but I didn't know the scripture so after prayer, I would google it or grab my Bible and look up the scripture, so then I connected to **Colossians 1:11** where it says, "Strengthened with all might, according to his glorious power, unto all patience and longsuffering with joyfulness.

Yes! It is just that simple. Sometimes in prayer a certain word or phrase would come to you that you never heard or may have heard before, and just so happen the Lord wants you to know that scripture for a reason.

Intentional time with God is not just limited to prayer but it can be reading a book on prayer, intercession, building relationship with God, leadership, current world events, or studying cultures. Reading, researching and retrieving information is useful in prayer. Information is the one thing that I assure you, prayer agents, is one of your weapons of mass destruction. The Bible says in **Hosea 4:6 AMP, "**My people are destroyed for lack of knowledge [of My law, where I reveal My will].

What is so key in this scripture is "the people". The destroying of the people comes from lack of knowledge. Can you imagine the destruction we can do with knowledge, revelation and information?
If the people would spend intentional time with God we could override destruction. Time spent with Him will allow us to receive information needed to devour, destroy, and demolish the adversaries of this world. As mentioned before, it is in His presence where we receive all we need. Prayer agents are deadly weapons all by themselves. We are a hub of revelation knowledge, spiritual illumination, and receptacles who are poured into and dispense out at the pleasure of the Lord Jesus Christ.

Prayer Experience

One of the experiences I had during our 21 days of fasting and prayer, God placed the building of the church inside of my belly. During prayer I could not stop rubbing my belly in a circular motion while travailing and weeping. As I continued to cry out, I kept hearing apostolic power and apostolic authority for the eastern hemisphere. I have never heard that before and honestly thought it was super weird. However, I was so far into the realm of the spirit that there was no room for second guessing. Unfamiliar with the eastern hemisphere, I grabbed my computer, searched the world map, and I called out in prayer all 197 countries in the eastern hemisphere. Lord knows, I was not fluent in pronouncing the names of these countries, but I was encouraged in knowing the Lord will make up the difference. It was for me to obey the voice and instruction of the Lord. I hit a vein when I begin to pray for genealogy of generations dealing with genocide. The spirit of the Lord began to show me what was occurring over there such as capital punishment. I saw in the spirit a young girl waiting to receive her punishment and I cried harder. The spirit of the Lord was telling me that my intercession spared the life of this young lady who was set to be murdered. Deep, huh? Imagine how I was feeling while in prayer. The prayer for the eastern hemisphere lasted over an hour and I mean it took everything inside of me. My vocal cords were getting tired, my back was feeling pain, stomach muscles felt like I did three hundred sit-ups, but it took all of that to pray forth the WILL of God for that region.

Remember, had I not sought-after God in prayer, this assignment just may not have been given OR the Lord would have given it to someone else. I am so grateful that He chose me to be the vessel to use at that time.

Prayer experience

From 11:03 p.m. (Monday, February 4, 2019), I was compelled to pray in my living room. I kept hearing to light a log of fire in my fireplace, but I knew that it would burn for 3 hours. I did not plan to be up praying that long. I realized 11pm was the second hour of the second prayer watch. I started to research what occurs during the second and third watch of prayer as well as locate scriptures to pray.

I lit the fire, grabbed my tallit, laid my white prayer sheet on the floor and began praying in tongues. The tongues I spoke were in different textures and sound. I was accelerating in speed while speaking in my heavenly language so much so that I could hardly catch my breath. I continued to speak in heavenly tongues while lying on the floor by the fire. In the last hour of prayer, I then began to sing songs from Psalms 43 and I also begin creating my own song: "I will sing of your love forever. Your name is mighty. Your name is holy … Your name is above all other names."

At midnight I began to tell God, "I am here, open and willing to be used by you. Speak to me, Holy Spirit." I began to cry and speak in my prayer language again. As I was praying in tongues, I heard God say, "Keep coming. Keep coming toward me and enter into my presence." Fear was on me, but I kept going. I felt lifeless, but I kept going. It was a time of silence. God did not show me anything nor did He say anything else. I just heard the fire going as I remained still. I got up and laid on my couch, wrapped in my tallit, and fell asleep … or so I thought. I woke up at 3:07 a.m. The fire was still burning. I began walking the floor for a few minutes continuing to pray. After that I sat on my couch and watched the fire continue to burn. It was then that I knew that God was showing me something about the fire. In the beginning stages I could barely light the log as the paper burned quickly but the fire just barely scorched the log. It was a slow start but when it did catch fire, it lasted longer than the manufacturer advertised. My prayer at that moment of revelation was – "Lord that is how I want my fire for you to be." I want my prayer life to exhibit that same type of experience.

I then begin to pray for the Lord to consume me, provide me with the fire I needed. Go down in my belly and put a zeal, an anointing, a longevity and perseverance within me. Give me a hunger and appetite for prayer and intercession that never goes out. As I prayed the spirit of the Lord took over me. I then asked for miracles, healing, deliverance, power, and authority to be placed in my belly and reveal mysteries to me like you did to those ancestral intercessors. Give me the power, the well of knowledge like you released to those in the Bible days and those you have released it upon on earth. The mantles you placed on those who were once in the earth like A. A. Allen, Mother Estella Boyd, Katherine Kuhlmann, Bishop Charles H. Mason, Lord give me that same mantle. It was a mantle of healing, prophecy, miracles, signs and wonders.

After praying that prayer, I was then sent into meditation. The fire went out sometime between 4am-5am.

The experience was a teachable moment for me with the Lord and that was for me to learn how to be still, how to light a fire that goes out on its own timing. The spirit of the Lord did not speak to me with instructions on anything. He just wanted to me to be still in his presence and receive revelation. WOW! What a powerful experience.

Father I pray for every intercessor, prayer agent, praying people all over the world reading this book. Bring us back to the place where your presence is made priority over everything else. Father to know your Will is all we should desire in the inner most part so teach us how to hunger after your Will. Lord I come against the mindset of being absorbed with our day to day tasks in life that we negate the fact that your kingdom business cannot be alienated but must continue to be established in this earth. Lord you called us to this life of prayer, this life where you are Lord overall. The Bible says this earth is yours and the fullness thereof, so God we repent for thinking this world belongs to us and how we try to do life without you. Father God, train our ears to want to hear your heart, open our minds to receive your thoughts, and deliver us from stagnant behaviors. Father, we want to advance your kingdom here and we are ready to be what you have called us to be. The Bible says creation is waiting for the manifestations of the sons of God. We must be in alignment, in position and in our seats of authority in heavenly places with you. In order for us to maintain our seat, we must stay in the place of your presence, always wanting, always hungry, always seeking so that we can see a move of God in this world. Use us Lord for your kingdom, IN JESUS NAME, AMEN.

―――――――――――――――

"But no one can go into a strong man's house and steal his property unless he first overpowers and ties up the strong man."

-Mark 3:27

―――――――――――――――

Prayer Assignments: What to Pray For?

Prayer assignments are vehicles used to release heavenly results on earth. The word "*assignment*" is defined by Webster's dictionary as "an *allocation of a job or task*". Prayer agents have an obligation in prayer to fulfill a task which is to seek the Lord concerning the need in the earth. The support we as prayer agents have from heaven is found in Matthew 18:18 **AMP** I assure you and most solemnly say to you, whatever you bind [forbid, declare to be improper and unlawful] on earth [f]shall have [already] been bound in heaven, and whatever you loose [permit, declare lawful] on earth [g]shall have [already] been loosed in heaven.

The principle God has given us is the ability to <u>BIND</u> and to <u>LOOSE</u>.
Jesus assures us that when we enter prayer that whatever we bind on earth heaven will back us up. We have a support system and agreement with heaven. My GOD. If I bind up poverty in my family bloodline, then heaven says, "Okay, let's bind it up." I cannot just bind it up, though. I must replace it with something. Therefore, I then loose financial increase on earth and heaven says, "Alright. Let us do it then." THANK YOU, FATHER! Prayer agents, did you read what I said? We can bind up and loose anything by faith in the name of JESUS and then he will answer us.

Let us go deeper with this scripture as it pertains to prayer. One thing to keep in mind as you pray, is to give direction to the spirit you are binding. Meaning if we bind a spirit where does the spirit go? What kind of spirit are we loosing to occupy the space? Think about this, if a robber breaks into your home and you capture him, tie him up to the point he can no longer move. What is the next step? Will you allow the robber to stay bound up in your home? Of course not, you call in the authorities to arrest him and they will whisk him off to jail to receive further counsel. Let us say the robber had an accomplice who got away and took some of your items in the home. The next step in your discovery for restoration is to file an insurance claim to replace what was missing. Whew, this is blessing me.

Prayer works the same way. Take a look at Mark 3:27 for further scriptural support.

We begin in prayer by seeking God concerning the spirit we are to bind. We then ask God to show us the strong man of that spirit.

While this is happening in our prayer, heaven is responding to us by binding the spirit and exposing by revelation the strong man.

Next, we give the spirit a place to go after it has been identified and bound. We find in scripture according to Matthew 12:43 "Now when the unclean spirit has gone out of a man, it roams through waterless (dry, arid) places in search of rest, but it does not find it.

Using this scripture for support, we send that spirit on assignment to dry places where it has no authority, no power, and no rest.

We then loose the spirit of God to take residence within the open space. For example, if we bind up fear and send it to dry places, we loose the spirit of faith. We apply scriptures on faith in prayer and give the spirit an assignment while it is taking residence. The spirit of faith will cause the open space to build upon trust, patience, belief, and hope.

Meditate on this passage of scripture for an additional thought:

John 14:11-14

Believe me that I am in the Father, and the Father in me: or else believe me for the very works' sake. Verily, verily, I say unto you, He that believeth on me, the works that I do shall he do also; and greater works than these shall he do, because I go unto my Father. And whatsoever ye shall ask in my name, that will I do, that the Father may be glorified in the Son. If ye shall ask any thing in my name, I will do it.

There you have it! Faith (belief), asking (prayer), praise (glorify the Father), manifestation (I will do it) are all found in this scripture. There is so much to pray for, but it helps when you know what to pray. A prayer assignment gives insight on the purposed plan of God for your life and the lives of others. If I need physical healing, then praying an assignment of financial increase is not the proper direction I need to go. When prayer agents are given a prayer assignment, it is guaranteed to get God's attention and will yield a result. Here are a few common ways that prayer assignments are released:

1. Given by the prayer agent
2. Given by the Spirit of God
3. Given by leadership

Assignments created by the prayer agent could be based upon a burden at a particular time, current events, or pressing circumstances that require immediate attention from Heaven. For example, the government experienced a shutdown on December 22, 2018 which caused thousands of people to be without jobs. The impact of the governmental shut down was overwhelming and unexpected. Many people experienced feelings of hopelessness, financial insecurity, confusion and more. I am inclined to believe it was prayer agents throughout the world who stayed in prayer for this release to occur. January 25, 2019 the governmental shutdown ended, and jobs were restored. To God be the glory!
Using this moment in the history of our world, a prayer agent would pick this up in the spirit of God and make a prayer assignment to pray it through until there is resolution.
There are times the spirit of the Lord will give an assignment to pray as well. When the spirit of the Lord gives a prayer agent an assignment, it is simply because there is an urgency in the realm of the spirit.

Just as in the earth, when there is an emergency, 911 is called and help is immediately sent to the location of the crisis. The same concept applies in the spirit realm. The Lord says, "Alright. There is something happening in the earth that needs my attention, my glory, and my word." However, it must be revealed to those who will seek Him in prayer. Another reason why the spirit of the Lord will give an assignment is for his Will to be manifested in the earth and needs a conduit to pray it through.

In Matthew 9:36-38 Jesus was healing and casting out demons under the power of the Lord. There were crowds of people needing to be healed, encouraged, and seeking answers. Jesus was doing the ministry work alone but knew that more work was needed in this region. It was not His assignment to stay in that region because there was more that he would have to encounter on his journey. Therefore, he knew once he was removed from this place, the people would still need to be ministered to with guidance and instruction. He then gave the disciples a prayer assignment by saying pray to the Lord of the harvest that workers will come forth and work in the field. The assignment was specifically tailored to the need of the people. The Lord had a need for people who could jump in, take over, operate in His authority, and harvest souls. This is where prayer agents arise. We call prayer agents to receive assignments from the spirit of God. The Lord will not release an assignment that He does not have need of. If the spirit releases it, there is a definite need, and He is charging you to pray it through until the point of delivery.

<u>Prayer Experience</u>:

I was in prayer and as I began to speak in my heavenly language (tongues), the Lord showed me a vision. The vision was of a place that was in ruins. In the vision this place had no color. It was completely uninhabitable and looked as if it had been burned down. I seemed to be on a mountain overlooking a city, and I was pointing to an area that was in a far distance. In the vision, the spirit of the Lord was standing there with me. God then said to me, "This is how the church looks. It is in a bad looking state and doesn't have my presence." He began to share with me that the church is camouflaging a look that is not how it appears in the spirit. Meaning, what we are showing the people is not what the Lord sees.

I heard him say to me, "Just as the heartbeat has rhythm, synchronization and a pace, this is how I see the church. It is on life support because the heart has been overworked and strained by too much pressure pulling on it. The oxygen needed to flow to the heart is stifled and clogged causing the heart to eventually lose its strength."

I began walking down to the place of ruins and I saw people. Everything around them was black and white. However, they were in color and imprisoned. I saw a little girl and preachers behind gated bars of burned iron. What was so surprising is that these people were happy and rejoicing as if the work they were doing was satisfactory to the Lord. It was as if they were oblivious to the fact that they were in color, living in a non-colorful world and behind bars. As I continued to walk, I saw a light in the sky with wings stretching out from it. It was the eye of God looking over this place. The Lord then had me pray for the minds of these people so that He could bring them out of bondage, and they be open to receive revelation from Him. He shared with me that many have strayed away from the gospel of Jesus Christ to establish their own truths. God said during this time, the apostolic order is coming to re-establish the church back to its original intent. I began to pray for truth to be revealed as he instructed.

As I type this experience, my heart begins to grieve all over again. There is so much to unpack from this prayer experience:

(1) the state of the church being viewed by God as a place in ruins.

(2) being happy about operating in color behind bars, but the world around you are void of color.

(3) God sees the church as his heartbeat, meaning that He is on one accord, one rhythm, one sound with the church He created, but the church is negatively impacting the heart.

(4) and finally, how the church is viewed in the earth to one another is not how God sees it. Lord, help us. The Lord showed me this detailed vision so that I can have knowledge on what to pray for. I had to pray for the mind, the WILL, the spirit of the church to match the spirit of God – praying that the church, the ecclesia would fall back in love with God and love him just as much as he loves us.

While praying on an assignment, the spirit of the Lord may route you to another lane, level, place, location, or dimension. This can also be referred to as prophetic intercession. Prayer agents may not be office prophets or operate in the office of a prophet, but the more you pray, the clearer you begin to hear from God. For example, one may pray for a family member and while praying the Lord will shift your prayer to financial increase for a business in another state. What does that have to do with your family member? While you are still praying, it seems as if you hit a "vein." It is like you are praying, and you get stuck in this one place and cannot progress from this topic or area because the spirit of the Lord takes over. It is at that point you are entering into prophetic intercession.

Prophetic intercession causes you to pray what you hear, see, smell, feel, and even taste. The five senses, just like in the natural, are used spiritually and will shift you according to how it enters your spirit. This is a form of assignment in prayer by way of prophecy.

The Lord has an immediate target, focus, need, in a specific area and He is choosing to use you while in the anointing of God to flow freely to capture it. During prophetic intercession, the Lord begins grooming you, developing you, and training your senses to travel in the spirit through various dimensions, levels and realms. This is a process where you are no longer in control, but the Holy Spirit totally dominates you, becomes your tour guide, increases your faith, and strengthens you more in prayer.

Prayer Experience

The spirit had me to pray Ezekiel 37 – "the valley of dry bones" – and how it represented the state of the current church. I began praying for valley experiences that some individuals are having because the WILL of God required it to be (the Lord had to bring His people to a low place). I also prayed for those people who are in a valley place voluntarily (their minds, choices, and decisions warranted the response). In other words, it is a low place of hopelessness, low-thinking, and without momentum. I prayed that the members of the body of Christ would be fitly joined together again to accomplish the work of the ministry. The valley should not be a permanent place but a place of brokenness that leads to reparation, restoration, and revival.

I prayed (as I saw in the spirit) that the mountains positioned next to the valley would encourage and give hope to the people. A valley will never become a mountain; therefore, it is encouraging to see there is a high place, an acceleration, and a point of destination. As I prayed, revelation began to flow and reveal that executive and senior leadership was on top of the mountain. Therefore, I prayed for top-level leadership everywhere in the world and in every system of the world.

I was then led to pray for economics, financial services, financial analysts, accountants of all kinds and in all places. I prayed over government and politics as it relates to finances. I prayed for local ministries regarding proper allocation of funds. I prayed for people who have been hindered by giving in church and how some churches have caused closed heavens to be over them due to how they are misappropriating funds of the ministry.
I prayed for strategists and experts in the areas of economics, declaring when God fixes it in government,

He will fix it everywhere. AMAZING! This is a prime example of how prayer on one topic can immediately shift to a totally different subject led by the spirit of the Lord.

Keep your eyes and ears open, prayer agents, as you can NOT be comfortable praying one way on one topic always. The spirit will begin guiding you while you are in the realm of the spirit to pick up whatever is in your way. Let me offer you this view: if you are driving east to get to a destination, on your way there, you will pass several stores, homes, businesses, etc. Sometimes, while heading to your destination you may see something that you realize you either need, or desire. When you locate what that need or desire is, you take a moment to make a stop to retrieve that thing and once retrieved you get back in the car and proceed to your destination. Prophetic intercession is very similar. You begin praying for one thing on your journey to get the manifested promise of God released on earth, but he does not just want you driving with one place in mind. The Lord has need of you to pick up some items, people, places, complications, and problems or block some attacks along the way. YES, LORD!

I remember a time, back when I was a part of a music ministry. We were traveling home from ministering in another state when one of our members became suddenly ill. He was having a very hard time breathing, which caused us to exit the highway and pull into a local gas station parking lot not too far from the expressway. A few of us carried him off the bus to get some air. A car pulled up rather quickly beside the bus. A woman rushed out the car and came over to ask if she could pray for our sick member. Without hesitation, we said, "Yes!" Normally, we would have asked questions about the woman before she began praying for our member, but there was a peace within my leaders' spirit to allow her to do so.

As she began to pray, the member began breathing slowly, but his recovery was quick. The woman said she was leaving a preaching assignment and, while on the expressway, the spirit of the Lord told her to exit and go where our bus was parked. She had NO IDEA that there was a sick person on our bus (or what was occurring for that matter), but God sent her to us. She did not want to leave us her name or any information as she was stern that the Lord sent her to pray, fulfil the assignment, and depart. God always sends you what you need when you need it. At that moment, a stranger, who knew nothing about us, had the oil and anointing to heal a sick man.

Burden of prayer -What is in me to pray?

A burden (as it relates to prayer) is a thing that weighs heavy on the inside of you. The definition of burden can be described as *"the carrying of a heavy load."* Ever felt like something bothered you so much and no matter how hard you tried, it seemed as if it just would not go away until you had to address and release it? This is what I call a burden of prayer.

Let us look at how Nehemiah describes his burden in Nehemiah 1:3-4

3 And they said unto me, the remnant that are left of the captivity there in the province are in great affliction and reproach: the wall of Jerusalem also is broken down, and the gates thereof are burned with fire.

4 And it came to pass, when I heard these words, that I sat down and wept, and mourned certain days, and fasted, and prayed before the God of heaven.

In chapter 1 of Nehemiah you will see his prayer unto God concerning his repentance on behalf of himself and the children of Israel. Nehemiah picked up the burden based upon the news he received of the wall being torn down and the city being left in ruins (destroyed). When a burden is placed upon you, the reaction may result in weeping, travailing, crying, screaming, and put you in a feeling of grief, bereavement, or even mourning. It is a heavy weight that is felt on the inside of you and the only way for that burden to be removed or released is by prayer. Nehemiah endured his emotional time of sadness and turned that into supplication to the Lord. In chapter two of Nehemiah, you begin to see the action plan come into fruition when King Artaxerxes saw that Nehemiah was burdened down and sad in his countenance. Let me pause for a second. Sometimes there are seasons when the burden of prayer is so heavy on you that others can see it in your behavior, character, and persona. Everyone will not understand. It may even be perceived that your current circumstance was created by you, but it is the burden you are carrying. King Artaxerxes granted Nehemiah the permissible authority to return to Jerusalem and release his burden. It is so amazing how Nehemiah prayed to the Lord in chapter 1 and God did not respond back to him by way of the spirit but used the king to give him the response to his prayer.

Prayer Experience

The Lord had me to pray for the United States of America. I prayed for Washington, D.C. and for all of those who are serving in the White House to have the mind of God. I prayed that laws and declarations that were signed, and bills seeking to be passed, be reformed and aligned with God. I then prayed for the east coast. The Lord began to show me there was an unidentified strong man (spirit) there. I then prayed for the west coast. There is where I received the revelation as to why they are commonly faced with earthquakes and wildfires. It is because that region of the USA is the area that travails. The spirit of altering, vanity, performance and entertainment are there. However, God is charging that area to become His travailing region.

I got stuck on praying for the southern states. It is in those areas where pioneers and strong leadership were birthed and developed, yet there was a strong spirit of stifled education, racism still, and historical bondage. I prayed so hard and interceded that God will rise in the south. As I prayed, I heard the spirit growling in my home as it agitated the spirits that were near. Weird, right? But I kept praying. I prayed then for the Midwest and northern states as God begin to show me that this is a place of liberation and currency but strong in organization like gang affiliations. I had the power and authority planted in me to bind the strong man of deception and manipulation and that sense of belonging. The Midwest connects all the other parts of the US on the map.

Our current world leadership is operating under a rebellious spirit and just as they are leading the world, it displays that spirit is acceptable in all areas of the USA, be it business, church, or home. It is a loose spirit that is unto witchcraft.

We still must respect those who have rule over us as the Bibles says but bind the wild spirit that is seeking to dominate this world. We can combat it in prayer. If we rebel against leadership and leadership rebels against the world, then it continuously feeds that spirit.

Burdens can be felt in
- the mind
- the spirit
- the heart
- the body-internally or externally

The burden in the mind is where it seems as if you just cannot stop thinking about a person, place, or thing. At night you find yourself continuously thinking about whatever it is that bothers you and cannot shake the thought. It could very well be because the Lord is downloading information to your mind and desires that either you pray it through immediately or will cause you to continue to receive downloads from Him until it's time to birth it out.

The burden in the spirit is when your spirit is not at rest. It is inside of you like a baby in the womb. It leaps in your spirit like the baby inside of Elizabeth in Luke 1:41-44. It just cannot contain itself. The Lord will cause this burden to enter your spirit, giving you the responsibility to carry it until it is time of delivery. For example, sometimes it can be the vision of spiritual or world leaders and for the Lord to give them strength. There can be a burden in your spirit of mass deliverance, family healing, establishing of God's glory in the world or the church.

The burden placed inside of the heart can often feel like heartache, heartbreak, compassion, a deep love, grief, and so forth. It lies within your heart; therefore, you may find yourself weeping, crying, extremely sensitive, emotionally unstable and sometimes overly emotional. The Lord places this on your heart because it is very likely that He wants you to feel His heart toward the person, place or thing.

The burden in or on the body can possibly affect you physically. Have you ever felt sudden headaches, physical illness, physical pain, I mean things where it is not normal for you? Yes, this could very well be a burden as this is God's way of allowing you to feel the weight, state, condition of the person, place or thing. The thing is not to harm you but to align you with it so you can know how to fight it off, release it, and carry it to delivery.

Prayer agents, we have a work to do! Burdens are a part of the requirements, expectations, and working component of who we are. We are wired for burden bearing and must remain sensitive to the Holy Spirit as to what burdens we are to bear.

Matthew 11: 29-30 AMP

Take My yoke upon you and learn from Me [following Me as My disciple], for I am gentle and humble in heart, and you will find rest (renewal, blessed quiet) for your souls. [30] For My yoke is easy [to bear] and My burden is light."

The scripture makes it very clear that prayer agents, praying people, intercessors of the households of faith carry the burdens for the Lord which are light. There is no way for us to bear burdens for the Lord without Him.

Intercession Experience

One Thursday night prayer service, I arrived about 30 minutes early to have intimate time alone with God before others arrived. I positioned myself on the altar, wrapped in my tallit, and cried out to the Lord in my heavenly language. As prayer service began, I continued to agree in prayer with what was being released by our prayer leader. As I walked around the room, stirred up in prayer, I asked the Lord specifically what he would have me to pray. The Lord led me to
Isaiah 62:6-7 KJV:

I have set watchmen upon thy walls, O Jerusalem, which shall never hold their peace day nor night: ye that make mention of the Lord, keep not silence,
7 And give him no rest, till he establishes, and till he make Jerusalem a praise in the earth.

As I took the microphone, I began to pray just as I was instructed by the Lord, and then something hit me like a strong wind. My belly felt like it was on fire and I begin losing control of myself. My knees hit the floor and I continued to call out to Jesus, and the praying people in the room were praising God. The Lord began to speak through me in prayer: "Miracles of healing are coming, and we are going to get immediate results!" I began to call out various sicknesses commanding a cure to be released and for God to release miracles of healing. I continued to declare that people in the hospitals would get reversal of bad doctor reports and receive good reports. The spirit of God began to move in the prayer service like never before. I put the microphone down, and, in the spirit, I saw a lady laying on a hospital bed who just received bad news. The Lord had me travail in prayer, crying out for her and others who are in a situation that felt hopeless.

The next day, I received a phone call from my pastor, who shared words of encouragement toward me from the prayer on the previous night. She went on to express how the burden and spirit of intercession was on me and how the move of God was prevalent in the room. The pastor received a message that a very close loved one of hers was enduring a health challenge at the time we were in prayer. The words from the prayer the night before were recalled back to her mind and she really believed that because of our prayer service and how God led me to pray for healing, caused what should have been a turn for the worse to actually turn out for the better.

It is so key that when you intercede for the people that you HEAR CLEARLY what the spirit of the Lord is saying unto the churches (***Revelation 2:7***). Intercession causes you to start the course one way. However somewhere along the way the Lord will open up another route, portal, or dimension that was unplanned, unrehearsed, never before seen heard or mentioned of, so that he can manifest his power in its respective locale.

Prayer Targets

The google definition of a target is defined as "a person, object or place selected as the aim of an attack; something at which someone is aiming a weapon or other object." Prayer targets enable us through our communication with the Father. By this communication we hit the bullseye each time. For example, if we are praying for healing, then we are seeking God to release healing in all necessary areas. For our request to be relevant in this area, prayer agents should use accurate healing-focused scriptures, boldly come to the throne of grace according to Hebrews 4:16, and believe in the healing power of God.

The evidence of reaching an intended target shows:

a. When there is a shifting in the atmosphere where we pray

b. When we receive a response from heaven and testimonies are released

c. When we get that "can't stop it" syndrome throughout our entire body during prayer.

Prayer Experience

The lead intercessor from my church asked that I lead prayer service one Thursday night. As I was preparing for the prayer service, I began to seek the Lord concerning the strategy. It was not my desire to just grab the microphone and pray what I felt, or thought would be sufficient I wanted to be specific in what to seek the Lord for. It is my belief that prayer should be a journey from start to finish. Therefore, I came up with this format:

- Praise and Worship – Entry Point
- Prayer – Requesting from the Lord (*identifying goals/target/petition*)
- A Moment of Surrendering – Cleansing and Yielding (*second entry point*)
- Intercession – Picking Up and Carrying the Burden
- Deliverance – Transporting, Removal, and Restoration
- Praise – Sealing It with Affirmation and Confession.

As I approached the stage to lead the people in prayer, I followed this blueprint and the Lord manifested His presence mightily. During the prayer, a burden leaped into my belly to shift the prayer into full intercession, causing me to pray for our senior leadership of the church. Submissively to the guidance of the spirit my entire body went from a standing position to falling on my knees crying out to God as I interceded for our leaders. Utilizing my entire body, perspiring uncontrollably, and voice getting tired and worn, the spirit of the Lord was resting on me so heavily that it had to be birthed out in that moment without ceasing. The formality of our prayer service begins with the prayer leader praying for the first 15 minutes and then permit others to lead in prayer. But the Lord had another plan in mind, causing me to lead 55 minutes of the one-hour prayer service. When God places the burden on the prayer leader, it will sit on you until the point of delivery. The Spirit will place the anointing and as long as it's sitting on you, it will cause you to flow.

Side note: it is very KEY that every prayer leader understand that when the anointing is placed on you; there is a grace to flow and operate until it (the spirit and anointing of God) is removed.

If the leader asks you to pray for 15 minutes, and the spirit is still on you at the last minute of your allotted time, release the microphone and conclude your prayer unless that leader permits you to continue. The Holy Spirit is a gentleman, a teacher, and respects order. Therefore, the spirit may very well be upon you so heavy that you find it hard to conclude, but, again, there is an order and we as prayer agents must respect that order. Now, when the spirit lifts off you, that is the indication from Heaven that there is nothing left to say. If an individual continues praying while the anointing of God has exited, prayer has now become that of the flesh. Remember the scripture in Acts 17:28 mentioned earlier – "In Him, we live move and have our being." Prayer agents MUST be sensitive to the Holy Spirit, respect the order, begin, carry out, and complete the assignment at the command of the spirit of God.

Okay, let us return back to the prayer experience. At the conclusion of the prayer service, a few of those who attended provided me feedback expressing how they felt like we went on a journey from start to finish.
I never disclosed to them that God gave me a format for that service, but the spirit led everyone to be able to obtain knowledge of it

I would like to take a moment, to share a little more insight into this topic. As we are digging into locating prayer targets, we must be cognizant of the capacity we have in prayer. In comparison to the military, there are ranking orders that relate to power and authority.

- Lieutenant
- Captain
- Major
- General

Ranking orders such as these listed above are just a few positions we are going to highlight.

All have different ranking orders for a reason. Each rank has a level of responsibility, a capacity of leadership, and a style of training tailored to those who they are leading. With that being said if I recently joined the army, I am not to be considered to hit the battlefield on the first day without being prepared. It is not the culture of the military for a recruit to advance to a higher rank after one day of training or lack of training at all. It is not expected for a recruit, without insight, knowledge or understanding of the military's culture and uniformity, to come in and train other people. Therefore, the purpose of the recruit is to be trained, taught, and prepared on how to execute in proper order. A focal point in the military during the time of battle is to fight an enemy with the mindset of killing everyone, if need be, who is on the opposing team. Prayer targets require that you know your team (those who labor among you), know your enemy (those you are fighting against), and know who you serve under (Kingdom of God). Makes sense?

How about this example,
- Have you ever been asked to give one million dollars on the spot and all you had was $20 in your bank account?
- Have you ever been asked to drive a semi-truck without a CDL license?
- Have you ever been asked to fly a plane without aviation training or certification?

More importantly, did you answer yes to any of these questions and did you fulfill the request? I can almost assure you that the answers to these questions are, ABSOLUTELY NOT. Sounds a little bizarre right to ask someone to go into their bank account and withdraw one million dollars, drive a semi-truck with no prior experience or credentials, or fly a plane filled with passengers without any training and proper licensing. Prayer works very similar. In prayer, we cannot expect our teams, or those who are unfamiliar, ungroomed or unknowledgeable in prayer, to tap into certain realms, dimensions, or levels without training.

Targets must be set that are realistic to reach! There are times where we may not hit the bullseye, or it may seem impossible. But the more you condition, train, organize a strategy, and become diligent in your prayer life, you will begin to see more times the target is hit versus being missed. The good news is that when you miss the target, it is not time for discouragement and giving up. That is the time when you evaluate the target, review how it was missed, and offer a solution or different strategy to accomplish bullseye the next time around. Prayer agents are always refocusing, reflecting, and restructuring ways to ensure that we are always target hitters. Let us visit some common terminology heard during prayer service:

Travail: to labor with pain; to toil. (KJV definition),
Merriam-Webster Dictionary defines travail as:
A physical or mental exertion or piece of work: task,
effort. The work especially of a painful or laborious nature

Travailing requires some of the following:

- ○ Placement of burden
- ○ Birthing out a vision (new, current, former)
- ○ Birthing or calling forth miracles
- ○ Manifestations (more of God, more of his presence, more of his   glory)

Push
- ○ Vision
- ○ Past emotions (earthly realm)
- ○ Movement (to release something into the atmosphere or the Spirit of God)
- ○ Tilling the ground (water of seeds for seedtime and harvest)

Cry out

- ○ Weeping (city, nations, country, family, systems, repentance, guilt, burdens, relief, desperation, seeking more, wanting more etc.)
- ○ For vision (let us see, hear, operating in the five senses)
- ○ For miracles
- ○ For healing
- ○ For deliverance

We cannot ask praying people to travail in prayer who are not willing to experience spiritual encounters with God. Often you hear some of these terms in a prayer service and it goes way over the heads of some people. Rightfully so, because the terms used in prayer are vital to those who connect with God in an intimate way.

Consider this, man will never know what it is like to be a woman and vice versa. For men to hear words like "become pregnant, carry, and deliver the seed" is something we are unable to identify with. However, in the spirit of God language, vernacular, terminology that is used is made universal to the believer where the spirit will bring revelation. The spirit of the Lord unifies the body of believers causing us to be one household of faith.

Again, to gain the understanding of this language, it is revealed to those who seek the Father and connect to His presence. When people are not in a place to worship the Father, be transparent and vulnerable to his will, then we are unable to travail in prayer. Travailing is a seed and burden placed on the inside of you which resembles that of a pregnancy.

How about this, have you ever been so excited about something that you felt it "in your gut"? It was as if you could not wait till whatever this feeling was to come to pass. The only information you could go off of was that it is something on the inside of you that is bringing forth excitement in your emotions. As time progress, when it reaches the point of revealing and you receive this gift or whatever it may have been, that the feeling leaves the body. Travailing gives you that same kind of feeling.

Intercessors are always seeking a burden and desiring to pick up something from the spirit realm. Their wombs should always be eager to have a seed inside of them to carry it out full term until its point of delivery. Ask the Lord what are you to intercede for?

What is happening in the world today, Lord, that I should take up a travailing, push or cry for?

Prayer Maps

I am super excited to share this part of the book with you. The Lord revealed this topic to me one day in the spirit and it has stuck with me ever since. The inspiration behind creating prayer maps, derived from tools crime investigators and the FBI use to solve crimes. In this part of the book we will explore how crime mapping is implemented and how it connects with the kingdom of God.

Wikipedia.com gives insight on **crime mapping. Crime mapping** is used by analysts in law enforcement agencies to map, visualize, and analyze crime incident patterns. It is a key component of crime analysis and the CompStat policing strategy. Mapping crime, using Geographic Information Systems (GIS), allows crime analysts to identify crime hot spots, along with other trends and patterns

Thoughtco.com says: Crime mapping identifies not only where the actual crime took place, but also looks at where the perpetrator "lives, works, and plays. Crime analysis has identified that most criminals tend to commit crimes

within their comfort zones, and crime mapping is what allows police and investigators to see where that comfort zone might be.

INCREDIBLE!!!!! Although the information listed above speaks to crime in our world, it runs parallel to that of spiritual things. The Bible says in
1 Peter 5:8-9 KJV,

"Be sober, be vigilant; because your adversary the devil, as a roaring lion, walketh about, seeking whom he may devour: Whom resist steadfast in the faith, knowing that the same afflictions are accomplished in your brethren that are in the world.

What is a prayer map? It is a visual board that contains territory, geographical locations, names, photos, directional points, and all necessary specific details that can be called out during prayer.

Prayer maps require researching information as it pertains to the demonic forces prevalent in those areas and to seek after the stronghold (strong man) that is dominating what you're praying for.

Establishing a prayer map causes us to know what houses we are entering into and once we get there what we are to do next.

It gives us insight as to what we are to pray against, what to bind up, and what to loose. Prayer maps causes prayer agents to operate according to **Jeremiah 1:10:** "*See, I have this day set thee over the nations and over the kingdoms, to root out, and to pull down, and to destroy, and to throw down, to build, and to plant.*

As I began to research the city of Chicago (as it pertains to the violent crime rate), I began to discover that not long after it's establishment, there was deception, manipulation, theft, and greed. The first gang in the city of Chicago originated from immigrants of other countries who migrated here and took residence in various parts of the city. As years went by, the political office had become corrupted by former gang members and leaders along with one of the world's most notorious gang leaders Al Capone who was dominate in running the city.

The bloodshed that took place between rival gangs, bank robberies, and political foes took the lives of countless young men. Many of those young men that died were affiliated with gangs and were under 30 years of age. According to encyclopediaofchicago.com, young males as young as 12 years of age were accumulating a rap sheet of imprisonment and committed murders on a consistent basis. This explains why from the 1800s to present day, the city of Chicago has experienced many unidentified snipers, gang rivalries and retaliations, lack of respect for city officials, and much more.

This is great information for prayer mapping as prayer agents all over the world can create a view of where these crimes have taken or is taking place. History plays a huge part in mapping out and bringing revelation as to why these areas are experiencing this kind of behavior in present time.

Prayer maps are great to be utilized when praying and interceding for:

o   Cities and states
o   Regions and territories
o   Families
o   Churches and reformations
o   Systems of the world
o   ministry assignments: evangelists, preachers, teachers, apostles and prophets
o   Nations and countries
o   Crime, murder, suicide and genocide.

It is my suggestion for every prayer person, leader, team, or group to create a prayer map. Traveling evangelists, prophets, apostles, musicians, and singers (whatever your ministry gifts are), I encourage you to research the areas and regions you are sent on assignment to minister PRIOR to your arrival. Enter these regions with foreknowledge, so that once you arrive, you are fully prepared for what you will potentially face. There are places in the earth that have such a strong demonic presence that if you are not careful, or knowledgeable, it will attack the believer so strongly that it becomes challenging to minister. Have you ever felt tired before or even after you minister? Ever been in a room and felt like you can't breathe, or your vocal cords are not cooperating properly? It could very well be that the spirit assigned to that region prepared an attack on you before you arrived.

Understand this brothers and sisters, just as the kingdom of God has an assignment, order, rank, weight and administration, so does the enemy. Therefore, if we create prayer maps, research regions, receive insight and foresight into what lies ahead, you better believe the enemy has trained his camp to do the same. Let's look to the word of God for support:

Matthew 12:25-29-Unity in the Kingdom of God and Satan

Knowing their thoughts Jesus said to them, "Any kingdom that is divided against itself is being laid waste; and no city or house divided against itself will [continue to] stand. [26] *If Satan casts out Satan [that is, his demons], he has become divided against himself and disunited; how then will his kingdom stand?* [27] *If I cast out the demons by [the help of] Beelzebul (Satan), by whom do your sons drive them out? For this reason, they will be your judges.* [28] *But if it is by the Spirit of God that I cast out the demons, then the kingdom of God has come upon you [before you expected it].* [29] *Or how can anyone go into a strong man's house and steal his property unless he first overpowers and ties up the strong man?*

I want to pause here for a quick minute. Reading these scriptures are so insightful and provide much information on the war we are fighting. Lucifer was an angel in heaven, who began to exalt himself. He had so much influence of power that one third of the angels were corrupted, converted, and connected to his spirit that when he was cast out of heaven, they went with him.
The angels he influenced were JUST LIKE HIM, due to how he was able to persuade, manipulate, and deceive them into following his lead. So, understand this: we are not dealing with an amateur or ignorant spiritual opponent. We are combating a skillful, and creative administrative traitor.

Lucifer (Satan), is very well aware of the ranking order, word of God, power and authority in how heaven is ran because he was a top tier leader in the heavens. In order for us to be successful in our attempts to combat the enemy and his camp, we must learn the order of God, the word of God, and the orchestrated plan of God.

The angels that were cast out with Satan have just as much insight as he does. Remember, they, too, were in heaven alongside of him. I am sure information sessions, trainings, manuals and more were put in place when they reached the pit of hell. The enemy is going to use every tactic, plan, scheme possible that replicates and duplicates what the Lord is doing in the heavens. Trust me, WE CAN NOT FIGHT THIS ALONE, but we MUST have the Holy Spirit on our side and within us to accomplish this warfare. The Bible says we are warring a good warfare. (*I Timothy 1:18).*

Fighting in the spirit:
For our struggle is not against flesh and blood
[contending only with physical opponents], but
against the rulers, against the powers, against the
world forces of this [present] darkness, against the
spiritual forces of wickedness in the heavenly
(supernatural) places

- Ephesians 6:12-AMP

For though we walk in the flesh [as mortal men], we
are not carrying on our [spiritual] warfare according
to the flesh and using the weapons of man. 4 The
weapons of our warfare are not physical [weapons
of flesh and blood]. Our weapons are divinely
powerful for the destruction of fortresses. 5 We are
destroying sophisticated arguments and every
exalted and proud thing that sets itself up against
the [true] knowledge of God, and we are taking
every thought and purpose captive to the obedience
of Christ.

-2 Corinthians 10:3-5-AMP

Prayer Focus

Focus is defined as "the center of interest or activity and to pay particular attention to." According to Webster's dictionary.

The scope of view becomes narrow to focus in on a specific assignment. The prayer map gives us endless possibilities of targets, information, places, people, and things we can cover in prayer; but the prayer focus diminishes those opportunities to a smaller view. For example, the map shows there is an overhaul of suicide in a city, but the focus will narrow the search from a city to neighborhoods, streets, businesses, etc. The prayer focus says, "Alright, I want to target this spirit in this specific area and will not ease up until I see a manifestation of God's power, will, and glory." As mentioned before, 2 Corinthians 10:3-5 is a guide on what we are facing in the spirit realm. I want to shift your attention to 2 Corinthians 10:4 KJV:

"For the weapons of our warfare are not carnal, but mighty through God to the pulling down of strong holds."

This is a perfect scripture to utilize for prayer focus as it provides us what to place our attention on and that is *STRONG HOLDS!* Identifying your prayer focus shows the reactive behaviors and energies that are in that region but knowing the "root" of the issue is super important. In most cases, the revealing of the strong hold(s) will be given by the spirit of the Lord while praying. The weapons (information, word of God, discernment, and insight) we use in prayer are mighty THROUGH GOD to the pulling down of strongholds. The scripture says, "mighty through God," which means that the strongholds can only come down through God.

So, when I get in the spirit of God, He enters into me. I then have the ability through my prayer focus to pull down the strongholds that are binding, capturing, and running free in those regions.

Prayer Agendas

We discussed developing a prayer map that outlines targets for prayer as well as creating a narrow view of focus. The next step in the process of prayer execution would be establishing a prayer agenda. *Agenda* by definition is "a list, plan, or outline of things to be done; a list of aims or possible future achievements." According to Webster's dictionary

Prayer agents should create a prayer agenda for themselves, prayer teams, or groups. The agenda allows the agents to visually see the journey, the order, the specific assignment to pray for and how long. Earlier in Part II, I made mention of the format (agenda) the Lord gave me for a Thursday night prayer service. Let us revisit it again:

- Praise and Worship – (*Entry Point*)
- Prayer – Requesting from the Lord (*goals/target/petition*)
- A Moment of Surrendering – Cleansing and Yielding (*next entry point*)
- Intercession – *Picking Up and Carrying the Burden*
- Deliverance – *Transporting, Removal and Restoration*
- Praise – Responding to the Seeking, *Sealing It with Affirmation and Confession.*

Regarding this agenda, it was just an overview of the journey we are taking for the one-hour prayer service. Notice, there is not a specific focus, time frame, or any specific details listed in this format, but there is a blueprint to follow and fill. Either way, this outline provides God's power to meet us according to these guidelines as this agenda requires and commands a move of God. At any given time, the spirit of the Lord can move in any line item listed for as long as He desires.

The Praise and Worship is the entry point in prayer where we focus only on God. We were not asking Him anything, but we devoted this time to adore, magnify, and become intimate with Him.

The Prayer (making our request made known) was for us to then share with God what we desire to see happen in this hour. We proclaim, confess, and prophecy our topics, focus, subjects and expect manifestations from the Lord to occur.

Moment of Surrendering is where we lay down emotions, leave the earthly realm, become completely detoxed, cleansed, and be vulnerable to Him. During ***intercession***, we are filled with the anointing, oil, and power of the Lord where we can now birth out, push out, pick up burdens, interrupt demonic attacks and more.

At ***deliverance***, we transport from the womb into the realms of the spirit where God has destined the thing to go. This can be considered a broken place, a shifting place, a place of removal.

In ***praise,*** we offer up for the victories we won, the plans that God intercepted, and the manifestation of things that have come and are yet to come.

Prayer agents, I want you to be fearless, precise, spiritual snipers in the realm of the spirit where you are so detailed and specific in your attacks. Have you ever heard of the seven mountains of influence? If not, no worries. I am going to provide you with insight on what they are and how this can be an agenda you may want to implement with your fellow prayer agents and/or agencies.

1. Government
2. Media
3. Business
4. Family
5. Education
6. Religion
7. Arts and Entertainment

For those who may struggle with creating agendas in prayer, the seven topics listed above are great starting points. Think about it – all these areas influence our entire nation, world, and earth in one way or another.

Consider this for a prayer agenda. In praying for government, we will cover the following:

- President and First Lady of the United States
- White House Staff
- Government Funding
- Governmental Laws

From these four areas, feel free to create an agenda where you can pray it through until the Lord releases you to shift.

The seven mountains of influence are a sure go to when you are searching for something to pray. There are many devices that are contaminated in these systems by the enemy that needs to be cast down. It is not by accident that the word "mountain" describes what these areas are sitting on. The higher these areas are magnified the greater the warfare between good and evil, and heaven and earth.

March 2020, the entire world experienced a global virus known as

COV-19 (corona virus). As this deadly virus spread throughout the US and abroad killing thousands of people, it had taken authority in interrupting our day to day functions. Everyone in the world was impacted.

When you look at the seven mountains of influence that keeps our world functioning, you can see how during this pandemic not one of these were exempt from impact. The mountain of Media grew due to the way media was utilized before. Music concerts, religious services, and even outdoor gatherings had to be done via media outlets.

The mountain of education impacted graduating seniors who were unable to participate in their senior prom, graduation and various celebrations. Students leaving the school buildings abruptly and now learning how to homeschool via internet.

With so much occurring in the world, this is a time where prayer agents rise up and cover these areas. There are many hurting people who lost family members, jobs, unable to meet financial obligations, and more. God will use prayer agents all over the world to ensure we lift these areas up in the spirit of God and release the kingdom of God. *Revelation 11:15 says the "the kingdom of this world, is become the kingdom of our Lord and of His Christ."*

At the time of publishing this book, we are still in the midst of the pandemic, but I believe God for a total healing in our world. God will restore all that has been lost and will provide us with more than what he had prior to this pandemic.

PART III

Benefits of Prayer

As we are approaching the close of the book, I want to share with you the benefits of prayer and the role of prayer agents. **Psalms 68:19** says, *"Blessed be the Lord, who daily loadeth us with benefits, even the God of our salvation."*

The word that sticks out to me is *"loadeth,"* for it means we are fully supported, equipped, stored, and stocked daily. For praying people, this is a constant fueling that occurs in prayer even the more. How much more would God give to you, who seek Him and walk upright before Him? Praying people experience a level of warfare that some believers in Christ do not. Do you agree with that? The reason this statement is true is because those who seek a depth, length, weight, height, and tap into unknown spiritual realms in God will obtain a piece of Him that comes with a territory. Understand that the territory has opposing forces on those levels and in those realms assigned to sabotage and destroy all that God has put on the inside of you

I want to encourage the encourager, the seeker, the one who sows in tears but is left feeling like there is no reaping of joy. For those who feel like they are giving God everything but lacking in their personal life, know this: GOD HAS NOT FORGOTTEN ABOUT YOU. Let us look to the word of God as to how working for God will bring persecution, opposition, and even confusion but how victory is always won for the believer. Acts chapter 16 gives us the story of Paul and Silas who were on a journey of evangelism for Jesus Christ. As they are traveling to their destination, the enemy sends one of his vessels to distract them from their purpose:

Acts 16:16-17

And it came to pass, as we went to prayer, a certain damsel possessed with a spirit of divination met us, which brought her masters much gain by soothsaying: [17] The same followed Paul and us, and cried, saying, These men are the servants of the most high God, which shew unto us the way of salvation. And this did she many days. But Paul, being grieved, turned and said to the spirit, I command thee in the name of Jesus Christ to come out of her. And he came out the same hour.

We find in this passage of scripture that Paul and Silas were in Philippi heading to Macedonia based upon a vision the Lord showed him earlier in this chapter. When they entered Philippi, they encountered a woman named Lydia who was a worshipper of God but known for business. The time of them speaking with Lydia was time they were going to spend in prayer with God but, it turned into ministry.

As they were leaving from the place by the riverbank on their way to Lydia's house, a demonic spirit inside of a woman followed them for many days mocking and provoking them. It was like it was determined to distract them from their purpose. Paul had just about enough, and he cast the devil out of this woman. When the men she was working for saw that there was no more profit from their prized possession, they immediately went to the council (magistrates or serjeants) to lie on Paul and Silas. You following me?

The Bible goes on to say that the magistrates and chief leaders beat them publicly, which caused shame and embarrassment, called them Jews, and threw them in prison.

Let us pause for a second for some good revelation. Prayer agents know that your presence in an atmosphere will cause enemies to meet you before you even get a chance to fulfill your assignment. That is enough to preach right there. Basically, let me agitate your spirit before you agitate mine.

The enemy wants to make you angry, operate in your flesh, and negate your assignment but he will never win. The spirit inside of her was tormenting them for days and would not stop

Secondly, the attempted attack will put an identity on you that is untrue. The enemy will deceive the people and deceive your mind into saying that you are somebody that you know God did not design you to be. Therefore, if you are not careful, you can fall into places you never intended on being because of the identity, stigma, titles that are placed on you. Be confident, prayer agents, and know that you are called by God to fulfill His purpose, His plan, and His will for your life and the kingdom of God. After being beaten, and being called Jews instead of Romans, these two did something out of the ordinary – they sang hymns and prayed.

Third point of encouragement for praying people is to use what God has given you in times of trouble. Prayer is what got you here and prayer is what will get you out. Remember that your prayer releases bondage, opens heaven, and will set the captives free.

The Bible said the other prisoners were listening to them and the earth began to shake so that the bands, the chains, and prison doors were loosed. When you go through trying times, it is all for the great release that is coming from heaven. You never go through anything and not come out without something different. I really believe by own revelation that the reason the earthquake happened, and the prison doors were opened, was not just because of the singing and the prayer. I believe it had a new anointing, a new fire, and a new sound. See, when you go through and you can still operate and function in the spiritual things of God, what you do in the anointing has more weight. My God, I feel the power of the Lord. Your sound changes, your look changes, what you sing shifts, how you praise is different. You got me?

Lastly, I want to encourage you NOT TO LOSE YOUR SONG OR YOUR PRAISE. During whatever you may face as a result of following Christ, know that when you tap into the spirit of God, you are destined to get results.

The Bible says it like this in **Psalms 149:6 KJV** – *"Let the high praises of God be in their mouth, and a two-edged sword in their hand."*

Whatever you do, prayer agents, always keep your mouths filled with praise and keep prayer in your bellies. The book of **Genesis 37:3-11** talks about the story of Joseph, the dreamer:

³ Now Israel loved Joseph more than all his children, because he was the son of his old age: and he made him a coat of many colours. ⁴ And when his brethren saw that their father loved him more than all his brethren, they hated him, and could not speak peaceably unto him. ⁵ And Joseph dreamed a dream, and he told it his brethren: and they hated him yet the more. ⁶ And he said unto them, Hear, I pray you, this dream which I have dreamed:

⁷ For, behold, we were binding sheaves in the field, and, lo, my sheaf arose, and stood upright; and, behold, your sheaves stood round about, and made obeisance to my sheaf. ⁸ And his brethren said to him, Shalt thou indeed reign over us? or shalt thou indeed have dominion over us? And they hated him yet the more for his dreams, and for his words.

⁹ And he dreamed yet another dream, and told it his brethren, and said, Behold, I have dreamed a dream more; and, behold, the sun and the moon and the eleven stars made obeisance to me.

¹⁰ And he told it to his father, and to his brethren: and his father rebuked him, and said unto him, what is this dream that thou hast dreamed? Shall I and thy mother and thy brethren indeed come to bow down ourselves to thee to the earth?

¹¹ And his brethren envied him; but his father observed the saying.

- Genesis 37:3-11

Here in this story we find three very key components we as prayer agents can learn from:

1. Receiving a mantle
2. God-given dreams (prophesies)
3. The manifestation of dreams

Receiving a mantle (as it pertains to this passage of scripture) is the coat made by his father, Jacob, and this mantle obtained many colors (anointings and gifts). The Bible says when the brothers saw this, they hated him more. Prayer agents, you all have a coat of many colors. The colors of your mantle may possess apostolic authority, prophetic insight, pastoral leadership, evangelistic teaching, and more. One thing all prayer agents have in common is the mantle of prayer! Whatever your mantle is and whatever the Lord has given you within your mantle, WORK YOUR ANOINTING AND WORK YOUR GIFT. The oil validated you!

If your brothers, sisters, or enemies are not showing hatred on the mantle you wear, it could be because you are not wearing it enough for them to see it. Mantles make your enemies upset, feel threatened, and powerless. The enemy knows that if a mantle is passed on to you, there is a new covering and anointing coming that will defeat every enemy.

God-given dreams (prophesies) were given to Joseph for the Lord to show him what lies ahead. Joseph, like many of us, made the mistake of sharing his dreams too early to those who he thought could handle it. Little did Joseph know that releasing the dreams to his brothers caused more hatred within them. When the Lord shows you by way of the spirit things concerning your future, you must protect it at all cost. Understand prayer agents, everyone will not be supportive of your dreams, your ministry, or your gift; therefore, it is so important that you hold on to the promises of God until the day of manifestation.

Joseph's dreams were fulfilled by the Lord even when it seemed as if it would not come to pass. He had to endure the brothers conspiring against him, being placed in the pit for the lies told on him from Potiphar's wife, and other moments that occurred in his life before he made it to manifestation. God wants his prayer agents to know that during the turbulent and persecuting times, He is going to manifest his promises in prayer for His people.

RECEIVE DELIVERANCE

Prayer agents are constantly praying deliverance over other people whether they are familiar or unfamiliar with them. Be encouraged in knowing that God's intention for His people is not to be bound while others are set free. Deliverance is our portion. **Proverbs 11:21**: *Though hand join in hand, the wicked shall not be unpunished: the seed of the righteous shall be delivered.* **Psalms 34:19** says, *"Many are the afflictions of the righteous: but the Lord delivereth him out of them all."* And **Psalms 40:17** goes even further: *"Even though I am afflicted and needy, Still the Lord takes thought and is mindful of me. You are my help and my rescuer. O my God, do not delay."*

Deliverance for Prayer Agents (Story of Daniel)

I want to take a moment a talk about the life of Daniel. In the book of Daniel 6:1-10, the bible says Daniel had an excellent spirit within him which led him to have favor with King Darius.

Prayer agents should exhibit and always possess a spirit of excellence and in all things.

The officials and those in the kingdom were not pleased with the favor Daniel received from the king. Sounds very familiar like the story of Joseph, right? With that being said, the officials had a target on impacting Daniel by interrupting his prayer life.

The goal was not to take his title, money, or possessions only his lifeline with God. In their minds, knowing this was a praying man it would challenge him to decide between praying to his God or obeying the laws of the land.

Ultimately, if he chose to disobey the laws of the land, then it could interrupt his relationship with King Darius which could "possibly" remove the favor on his life.

The enemy knows that you have an excellent spirit, a lifeline communication and faith-filled relationship with the almighty God. The reason why you are a prayer agent is because you diligently seek God on a consistent and consecutive basis. We are all guilty of not being 100% faithful to our God given assignment concerning prayer, but the Lord hears and honors the time we have committed to him both in the past, present and the future to come.

Since there is movement and momentum in the realm of the spirit as a result of seeking the Lord, it becomes a huge threat to your adversaries. The king, who had all authority in the kingdom, allowed the people to force his hand at writing a decree that no one can pray for thirty days. What I love about Daniel was he heard the news and still proceeded to pray. I believe because Daniel was a man of prayer that the following occurred:

1. When Daniel heard the writing was signed, he intentionally went into prayer.
2. He opened his windows facing Jerusalem so the people could see and hear him praying.
3. Daniel entered the lion's den unbothered, which means that the prayers he previously prayed were stored up for this moment
4. Daniel, by way of prayer and the testimony of God, caused the decree to be reversed.

Role of King Darius

- He gave Daniel preferential treatment.
- He believed the God Daniel served would deliver him.
- He came back expecting to see a testimony of what God had done when he called to him the next morning.
- He rewrote the law in the favor of God.

Prayer agents, you need a King Darius in your life! King Darius wasn't a believer in the God Daniel served but Daniel's life encouraged the king. When living a life that pleases God, others will see it and be inspired and encouraged. Your life is the testimony that can lead someone to desire the same God you speak about.

The king was also prophetic by saying to Daniel more than once that God will deliver him. The Lord did just that! What is so amazing is that the king then placed the families of those people who encouraged the initial decree to be placed in the lion's den. There is a reaping that takes place in what you sow. The law (King Darius's decree) was then rewritten where prayer was only to be offered to the God of Daniel for, he is a deliverer. YES LORD!

What am I saying? Prayer agents stay on the course of seeking God, the deliverer, and He shall answer your requests. The prayers that you are praying cover, protect, and interrupt things occurring now and in the future. Whatever was meant to occur or to cause harm will either be diminished or completely abolished because of your prayers.

Deliverance for Prayer Agents (Three Hebrew Boys)

Daniel chapter 3:12-18 talks about the story of Shadrach (Hananiah), Meshach (Mishael), and Abednego (Azariah), also referred to as the three Hebrew boys who were thrown into a fiery furnace for obeying the Lord their God.

Here again is another story of triumph for the people of God. Remaining loyal to God in all things will truly pay off. The comparison of this story is congruent to Daniel in Chapter 6 as they all (Daniel and the three Hebrew boys) were appointed as leaders in the province. The Chaldeans in this scripture were the people who came to the king to inform him that these three men refused to obey the decree that says that at the sound of the music, bow down and worship the golden image.

As the story goes on, we find the confidence and the authority lying on the inside of these three boys as they boldly proclaim that "God is able to deliver us." Let's look at Daniel 3: 17-18 in the amplified version " *If it be so, our God whom we serve is able to rescue us from the furnace of blazing fire, and He will rescue us from your hand, O king. [18] But even if He does not, let it be known to you, O king, that we are not going to serve your gods or worship the golden image that you have set up!"*

Prayer agents, when life is filled with much chaos, noise, problems and attacks from the enemy, that is the time to trust God the more. These men said to their enemy, in so many words, I am not afraid of whatever you do to us. The God I serve is "able" to deliver us from the furnace and from your hand. However, if he does not deliver us, we still are not going submit to your authority.

MY GOD this is so powerful. The confidence in God and their relationship with him, meant more to them than obeying the law of the land. We must be fully engaged with the Father, that no matter the outcome, God was, is, and always will be able to deliver.

Upon the obedience of their relationship with God, He came through and prevailed. GLORY BE TO OUR GOD!

Glory of God

Prayer agents are atmosphere shifters, climate adjusters, and environment establishers who release the glory of God in all places and things. When we pray, we call on the anointing, the power, the fire of God and He responds with His glory. The glory of the Lord fills us, assures us, captivates us, and much more. We (prayer agents) cannot pray and intercede for the glory and not be recipients ourselves. In 2 Chronicles chapter 6, we find Solomon finishing up an assignment given by God and that was to build Him a temple. It was purposed in the heart of his father, David, to fulfill this assignment but the Lord had other plans. David laid out the blueprint for his son, and Solomon made it come to pass. As the conclusion of the temple being built was approaching, Solomon takes a moment to dedicate the temple unto the Lord.

Let's look at a few verses of the prayer offered unto the Lord by Solomon...

2 Chronicles 6: 12-19 KJV

And he stood before the altar of the Lord in the presence of all the congregation of Israel, and spread forth his hands:

[13] For Solomon had made a brasen scaffold of five cubits long, and five cubits broad, and three cubits high, and had set it in the midst of the court: and upon it he stood, and kneeled down upon his knees before all the congregation of Israel, and spread forth his hands toward heaven.

[14] And said, O Lord God of Israel, there is no God like thee in the heaven, nor in the earth; which keepest covenant, and shewest mercy unto thy servants, that walk before thee with all their hearts:

[15] Thou which hast kept with thy servant David my father that which thou hast promised him; and spakest with thy mouth, and hast fulfilled it with thine hand, as it is this day.

[16] Now therefore, O Lord God of Israel, keep with thy servant David my father that which thou hast promised him, saying, There shall not fail thee a man in my sight to sit upon the throne of Israel; yet so that thy children take heed to their way to walk in my law, as thou hast walked before me.

[17] Now then, O Lord God of Israel, let thy word be verified, which thou hast spoken unto thy servant David.

[18] But will God in very deed dwell with men on the earth? behold, heaven and the heaven of heavens cannot contain thee; how much less this house which I have built!

[19] Have respect therefore to the prayer of thy servant, and to his supplication, O Lord my God, to hearken unto the cry and the prayer which thy servant prayeth before thee.

The Lord responds to Solomon in Chapter 7:1-3 by sending his glory:

Now when Solomon had made an end of praying, the fire came down from heaven, and consumed the burnt offering and the sacrifices; and the glory of the Lord filled the house.

² And the priests could not enter into the house of the Lord, because the glory of the Lord had filled the Lord's house.

³ And when all the children of Israel saw how the fire came down, and the glory of the Lord upon the house, they bowed themselves with their faces to the ground upon the pavement, and worshipped, and praised the Lord, saying, For he is good; for his mercy endureth forever.

The Lord then responds audibly to Solomon's specific prayer (offered in Chapter 6) in verses 15 and 16 of chapter 7:

Now mine eyes shall be open, and mine ears attend unto the prayer that is made in this place.

¹⁶ For now have I chosen and sanctified this house, that my name may be there forever: and mine eyes and mine heart shall be there perpetually.

THANK YOU, FATHER!

Here are a few areas I would like to highlight from this encounter:

- Solomon dedicates the temple to the Lord. There is a blessing forthcoming when you take the time to tell the Lord, "THANK YOU." I truly believe that when we get beyond working just to reach the finish line, then a moment of reflection, gratitude, and dedication should take place. Solomon's heart as he was nearing the completion of temple being built, was for the Lord to be involved throughout the journey from start to finish. Prayer agents keep God involved. Summon and invoke His spirit on every assignment, project, event, and service.

- Solomon was specific in his prayer request unto God for the purpose of the temple.

Let us look at part of Solomon's prayer in 2 Chronicles 6:24-25 KJV.

[24] And if thy people Israel be put to the worse before the enemy, because they have sinned against thee; and shall return and confess thy name, and pray and make supplication before thee in this house;

[25] Then hear thou from the heavens, and forgive the sin of thy people Israel, and bring them again unto the land which thou gavest to them and to their fathers.

How could God deny answering these requests from Solomon after him taking time to offer intercession on behalf of the people? This posture of prayer allowed Solomon to offer details, descriptions, and scenarios, in pursuit of a release from God. In Chapter seven, you will see how God responded just as specific to Solomon. Check this out:

2 Chronicles 7:12-14 KJV

And the Lord appeared to Solomon by night, and said unto him, I have heard thy prayer, and have chosen this place to myself for a house of sacrifice.

[13] If I shut up heaven that there be no rain, or if I command the locusts to devour the land, or if I send pestilence among my people.

[14] If my people, which are called by my name, shall humble themselves, and pray, and seek my face, and turn from their wicked ways; then will I hear from heaven, and will forgive their sin, and will heal their land.

What I love about this is the Lord regurgitated back to Solomon what he sought him for. As you read more of Solomon's prayer you will see how specific he was in request to the Lord concerning what he desired to see take place in the temple. The Lord then signifies his listening ear to Solomon by saying here is what I am agreeing to based upon your request.

What I really want to highlight is the mere fact of God responding to Solomon and result of his response.

- **<u>Fire came DOWN from Heaven</u>** – Prayer agents have the ability to reverse the laws of nature. It is a well-known fact that fire burns upward not downward. God can do what He wants to do when He wants to do it. The fire burning down into the temple was God's way of showing how I'm going to respond to impossible requests by doing something impossible. YES, LORD! When we pray fire down from heaven, surely, it's an indicator that we have hit a vein and target that reached heaven and it comes to consume us.

- **<u>Glory filled the room</u>** – When prayer agents pray, we release the glory of God. We not only just seek for the glory but a weight and rank of glory. The glory of the Lord filled the entire house where Solomon prayed and was so strong that the priest could not enter and those on the outside could not stand. What a powerful move of God. When the presence of God is near, you break your rank, title, position and submit to His glory. This type of prayer is what every prayer agent should seek to accomplish in prayer: a time for the glory to fill the people with His spirit and power; a glory that's so weighty that the people are on one accord, worshipping, praising, offering, seeking, and crying out to God.

- **<u>God responds audibly</u>** – God, being so amazing, took the time to set the stage for Solomon as he prepared to manifest His glory. In 2Chronicles chapter 6, Solomon positioned himself toward the temple, stretched forth his hands, and uttered words in prayer that moved God. The Lord honored his prayer position and language he offered and returned to him by sending fire and glory. Days later after the fire and glory came down, the Lord answered his request and said to him in so many words in 2Chronicles 7:12, "Now you have my attention and my eyes, ears and name will be with this place. If the people commit to the things you ask of me, I will answer them as you requested." What an encouragement to know that what you pray, God will attend to because of the position you submitted yourself to and with the right heart, spirit, and mind.

I really feel led by the spirit to encourage prayer agents everywhere to bask in the glory of the Lord. In the midst of chaos, confusion, distress, or whatever you may be facing, the glory of God will strengthen, encourage, and uplift you. I leave you with these scriptures to meditate on:

2 Corinthians 4:17-AMP

[17] For our momentary, light distress [this passing trouble] is producing for us an eternal weight of glory [a fullness] beyond all measure [surpassing all comparisons, a transcendent splendor and an endless blessedness]!

Romans 8:14-18 KJV

[14] For as many as are led by the Spirit of God, they are the sons of God.

[15] For ye have not received the spirit of bondage again to fear; but ye have received the Spirit of adoption, whereby we cry, Abba, Father.

[16] The Spirit itself beareth witness with our spirit, that we are the children of God:

[17] And if children, then heirs; heirs of God, and joint heirs with Christ; if so be that we suffer with him, that we may be also glorified together.

[18] For I reckon that the sufferings of this present time are not worthy to be compared with the glory which shall be revealed in us.

Prayer experience (Glory of God)

Thursday mornings at 9am, the Lord placed me in a season of prayer live via Facebook and Instagram. Every Thursday morning, I would take one hour to devote to prayer with me and the Lord. In most cases, my spirit was filled with the prayer focus for the 9am prayer on social media. Therefore, my time spent with God prior to that was just a time of intercession, worship, and connectivity with the Father. Understanding that prayer was going to happen live, I would take a few minutes during my personal prayer time asking for God to breathe upon the prayer focus.

On Thursday May 13th, the Lord led me to pray that we would find our identity. I felt the burden that there were so many people who are not operating in their purpose in life. As I was preparing to go live on social media, I said in prayer, "Lord increase the viewers and allow it to be double than last week's views." I then said "Lord allow the people who attend prayer to be open, transparent and honest in confessing they are struggling with their identity." "For every person who confesses, God speak to them and show them who they are."

The weekly viewers who attended prayer the previous week totaled about 40 people. The prayer this particular week increased just like I prayed. In addition to that, the testimonies that were shared with me were from quite a few people who tuned in informing me that they are now ready to progress. God had revealed to them who they are and what they are to do. Hallelujah!

REACHING YOUR DESTINATION IN PRAYER

Prayer agents become conditioned and flexible in the following areas:

- Adaptable to the voice of God
- Aligning with His plan and His will
- Accurate in the execution of God-given assignments
- Accomplish the vision and mission of the kingdom.

There are multiple ways to reach your place of destination. Having a focus and a target provides assurance on how you get there (direction) and making sure you get there (arrival).

Example: Traveling to a destination geographically, there isn't one set way to get there. To travel to Atlanta from Canada is not the same way as getting there from Chicago. An airplane is not the only available mode of transportation that will ensure an arrival to Atlanta. It is recommended to be the quickest method to take as it shortens the time and distance, but it is not the only way.

There are various means and modes of transportation to utilize as it pertains to getting somewhere. Keep in mind, depending on where you are starting from determines which direction(s) you are to follow. If the place of destination is in the south, and I'm starting out from the west, then what do I need to do in order to get south? What is the best transportation mode and direction, and how much time does it take to get there?

An airplane, or any aircraft, requires boarding the plane, taking off from destination, experience possible turbulence depending on the weather, and concludes with a landing. It cuts the time in half for some travel destinations because it doesn't have to encounter things like traffic as motor vehicles do. Buses, trains, and automobiles cause the travel to take more time than expected. However, they provide a more scenic route whereas you get a chance to experience nature and see the changing landscapes and structures as you pass through.

Bicycles and walking are the longest methods of travel for long distances. For a 180-mile trip depending on the destination, it would take days to complete.

All the modes and methods listed above have one thing in common: they all are designed to reach a designated point of destination.

Whatever the passenger decides to embrace to reach the final destination is based upon his/her preferred choice. A passenger who chooses to fly via airplane isn't more sophisticated than the passenger who takes a train. Let me offer you this thought as it pertains to prayer. The spirit of the Lord gave me this revelation one day in prayer.

Airplane Prayers: when you have an urgent need and know what you want to say to God. These kind of prayers sound like, "Lord, you are the God that specializes in the impossible, so therefore I'm going to seek you diligently with the word because I need you to move IMMEDIATELY." Prayer agents who offer *airplane prayers* are those who are very familiar with traveling in and out of the spirit, understand the boarding process, select the proper seats on the plane, and get to God quickly. These kinds of people don't mind going back and forth between destinations in the spirit until they receive a result. Airplane prayers are not for vacations and resting places but for the agent to hit the vein, the target, and the destination, and will not rest until there is a manifestation. Look at the Prophet Elijah in **1 Kings 18:41-44 AMP…**

"Now Elijah said to Ahab, "Go up, eat and drink, for there is the sound of the roar of an abundance of rain." ⁴² So Ahab went up to eat and to drink. And Elijah went up to the top of Carmel; and he crouched down to the earth and put his face between his knees, ⁴³ and he said to his servant, "Go up, look toward the sea." So he went up and looked and said, "There is nothing." Elijah said, "Go back" seven times. ⁴⁴ And at the seventh time the servant said, "A cloud as small as a man's hand is coming up from the sea." And Elijah said, "Go up, say to Ahab, 'Prepare your chariot and go down, so that the rain shower does not stop you.'

What is so awesome is the position of both Elijah and the servant. Elijah stayed in the position of prayer and intercession after he released the prophetic word to King Ahab that rain is about to come.

However, while Elijah remained in the prayer posture, he could not waste time seeing when manifestation was coming as that would possibly cause him to doubt.

Elijah, I'm sure, was saying, "Let me keep seeking because a word was released, and I have to pray this through until the Lord releases it." Therefore, the servant went six times to look and report back (boarding and unloading the plane), to see if the rain was coming. It was the seventh time where the servant went and there appeared a cloud. The cloud appearing was an indication that the rain was about to come, and the prophecy would be fulfilled!

The Lord gave the prophet a word and it was time-sensitive, therefore the only method (airplane prayer) he could take was get to God quickly.

<u>Bus, Train, and Automobile Prayers</u> – When you don't quite know what to pray or seek Him for, you can reach Him by bus, train or automobile, figuratively. What occurs on these modes of transportation is for prayer agents to be groomed and developed in the spirit of God. The methods of travel are designed to build up prayer agents visually and spiritually, causing time of preparation as to what to bring to God during your time of need. In looking at the natural purpose of these three, they each possess wheels that are used on the road or track. There is lane designation and definition for these methods. At times, prayer agents are in a place in God where we know we need to pray, or unsure of what God is saying in this season. Therefore, instead of becoming stagnant or enter into a season of prayerlessness, we enter into prayer, but we are pacing ourselves. The purpose of pacing ourselves is for us to learn more of Him. In the end, we will get to God and reach our destination; it just may take a little longer getting there.

---

⁴ Then the word of the Lord came unto me, saying,

⁵ Before I formed thee in the belly I knew thee; and before thou camest forth out of the womb I sanctified thee, and I ordained thee a prophet unto the nations.

⁶ Then said I, Ah, Lord God! behold, I cannot speak: for I am a child.

⁷ But the Lord said unto me, Say not, I am a child: for thou shalt go to all that I shall send thee, and whatsoever I command thee thou shalt speak.

⁸ Be not afraid of their faces: for I am with thee to deliver thee, saith the Lord.

- Jeremiah 1:4-8 KJV

What I enjoy about this passage of scripture is how relevant it is to most believers. God has put spiritual gifts within us, yet we lack confidence and feel as if the ability is not there. God is a god of time, order, season, destiny, and appointments. There are times He needs prayer agents to move quickly and with haste. Then there are times He just wants those who will be humble enough to say, "Yes, Lord. You called me but I do not know what to say or how to say it. So, show me, Lord. Guide me day by day Lord, so I can see You! Prayer agents enjoy taking the scenic route sometimes and do not be in such a hurry to fly all the time. There are times the anointing of God will come upon you to soar but then there are times you just need to sit back, view the land, smell the air, see the mountains and valleys, and He will speak to you.

Bicycle/Walking Prayers The final method of transportation is bicycling or walking. Simply put, this is taking your time getting to the place you are seeking to reach. Yes, it seems crazy mentioning these two, but they are super important to highlight. There are many prayer agents in the world who exhibit this mode. This is not a mode to diminish or to take negatively (although it can be), but it is the least likely to be chosen because it's takes so long to fulfill. Can you imagine living in Los Angeles and walking to Miami, Florida? Is it possible? Yes, it is. It will just take you several weeks to complete, but it can be done. Again, it is not a place to talk bad against as some of these characteristics could be upon prayer agents based upon previous experiences or lack of experience in general.

Now there are times when this route is taken due to disobedience and not submitting to the plan of God, which is the part that is not pleasurable to God. Yet, it still will bring God the glory.

Let us talk about the story of Jonah. In. *Jonah 1:1-10,* Jonah was given a word from the Lord and he did everything possible to hold the word inside of him. Instead of taking confidence using the airplane method or ponder it a little longer for clarity like the bus, train, and automobile method, he decided to get on a bicycle AND at times chose to walk, in efforts to avoid releasing this word. He soon discovered that everywhere he went to avoid fulfilling the word, was going to disrupt, distract, and cause confusion to those he would encounter. Eventually, Jonah had no choice but to get to his destination quick, fast, and in a hurry. It was only a matter of time before he would run out of options and had to fully submit to the plan of God.

Prayer agents, although this stage/mode can be for those starting out in prayer or for those who rebel against the fulfillment of the assignment, still come forth into the place where doing the work of the ministry is your primary focus. The Lord will not provide all the details, insight, or answers to every assignment He gives; but whatever is chosen by God for you to fulfill DO NOT STAY on this level too long. The destination must be reached and, according to the word of God in **Matthew 24:14,** *"And this gospel of the kingdom shall be preached in all the world for a witness unto all nations; and then shall the end come."* LET'S GO UP! Remember *"The Oil Validated You!"*

As mentioned earlier under this subject, adapting, aligning, accuracy, and accomplishment happens during this journey of reaching your assigned destination in prayer. Adapting to the voice of God happens out of obedience to moving in the spirit.

Adapting to His voice silences the voices of every demonic and illegitimate spirit that is not the voice of God. Prayer agents begin deciphering between the voice of God, their own voices, and the voice of the enemy. The Lord begins to speak in various ways and will move according to His desire at the time He speaks. The Holy Spirit will train your ear to hear, eyes to see, mind to think, and mouth to speak as you submit to His command.

Aligning with His plan and His will is super important in reaching your destination in prayer as the Lord, desires fulfillment of His word to be done. Aligning causes denial of flesh, opinions, reservations and hesitations. This process will give you a sense of ease as it follows the process of being adaptable to His voice. Prayer agents will hear God and then position themselves in full alignment with His spirit. Once you are in alignment, synchronized, on one rhythm and understanding with the Lord, connectivity and productivity can begin.

Accuracy in your God-given assignment occurs after you are adaptable to His voice and align with His will. The Lord can trust you now as you are in Him and He is then inside of you. The Lord can see Himself moving in His vessel and conduit, so there will be a fulfillment of the assignment. The more you move IN GOD, THE MORE you avoid the spirit of error, entertainment, self-kingdom building, and seeking validation and approval of man.

Prayer agents need to become bullseye hitters every time because you are trained, skilled, and anointed by God and under the hand of God to execute.

Accomplish the vision and mission of the kingdom is the final stage of reaching your destination. Once I become adaptable, align myself, become accurate in executing my assignment, I can then accomplish and move forward to the next phase and place in God. Ultimately, prayer agents want to hear from God, "Well done, my good and faithful servant," (**Matthew 25:21**). The Lord placed an emphasis on your task to bring His kingdom to come in the earth as it is in heaven (**Matthew 6:10**). Therefore, we have the finishers anointing on our lives to make sure we reach our destination and not only reach it but accomplish what we are assigned and charged BY GOD to do.

ROLE OF THE PRAYER AGENT

Throughout this book, the word "prayer agent" has been stated several times without a true explanation. The purpose of holding off this term until the final chapter of the book was for the reader to understand the journey, characteristics, and work associated with a truly souled out prayer life. I will start with a standard definition of *agent*:

Agent– an agent is any person who has been legally empowered to act on behalf of another person and obtains information that produces a specified effect.

When I was charged by the spirit to write this book, I immediately saw a vision of a detective an FBI or CSI agent on duty. It was as if they were identified not by how they look but what they do. When you look at a FBI or CSI agent, when they are on duty the apparel worn shows in oversized font the letters "FBI" OR "CSI". A detective carries a badge most times or you may see something on a jacket that will display DETECTIVE. However, when they are off duty, their job title does not change they are just not working at that time. Makes sense?

The Lord gave me the name "Prayer Agent" because it is comprised of praying people all over the world who are seeking the kingdom of God on a regular and will push the movement of prayer in the earth.

 The thought of it was interesting because just as there are legal authorities in the earth, so are they in the spirit realm. Individuals pray on earth but operate in the kingdom of heaven. We legislate laws, rewrite laws, enact laws … I mean you name it! And we have the power to make it happen.

Prayer agents are constantly doing the following:

- Praying and Prophesying
- Releasing
- Activating
- Yielding
- Empowering
- Renewing
- Aligning
- Governing
- Establishing
- Navigating
- Trailblazing

Praying and Prophesying are one of the main expectations and requirements of any prayer agent. We pray the WILL of God and release the prophetic word of God. Prayer agents always have the capacity to pray and prophesy. God is always speaking and desires to speak to His people.

Releasing means that we are letting go of our will, agendas, emotions, issues, and problems so that we can be filled with the spiritual things of God. Prayer agents release the oil, anointing, visions, dreams, and heart of God to His people.

Activating other prayer agents is the responsibility of the prayer agent. We impart wisdom, spiritual knowledge, word of God, protocol, and order. For the prayer agent to activate other agents, one must be under the anointing and power of God. One must be healed, delivered, and filled with the Holy Spirit to impart into others.

Yielding requires making way for the Holy Spirit to move and being sensitive to the spirit of God.

Empowering other agents to serve the Lord is an essential function of a prayer agent. We must be obedient to studying gifts, prayer languages, and all spiritual things.

Renewing our minds, spirits, heart and body consistently so we can continue to receive downloads from Heaven and to receive the mind of God concerning His people.

Aligning with the purpose, plan, and Will of God

Governing the kingdom of God, protecting the earth, and defending the gospel of Jesus Christ.

Establishing the kingdom of God on earth as it is in heaven, we make new laws, shift cultures and atmospheres.

Navigating other agents through realms of the spirit is essential so that they, too, can be navigational tools, compasses, and directional guides for others.

Trailblazing refers to those leaders who are the first to start a prayer assignment. They start paths to become mentors and strong leaders of influence to ignite a prayer movement.

In other words, we are the church that prays earnestly until the supernatural release occurs.

Acts chapter 12 talks about how Peter was in prison at the hand of King Herod who was planning to kill him in front of the people. However, the church began to pray fervently, on one accord, interceding for Peter. The prayers were so effective that the Lord supernaturally sent an angel to get him out of prison and no one seen him leave. As a matter of fact, no one saw the angel but Peter and even he was in a state of confusion. The story continues saying how Peter reached a place where the angel left him, he came to himself and said (in so many words) now I know nobody, but God could have done that.

Prayer agents, when we hear about captivity, murder, wrongful injustice, and persecution, it should stir us up to pray. Therefore, we are here in this earth to take the news, information, and research and bombard heaven until there is a great supernatural release. If we hear it, we are responsible to seek the kingdom of God to release angelic hosts in the earth. Hear me! We seek God until we see manifestation.

Later in this scripture, you will see Peter making his way to the house where the church was praying and Rhoda answered the door, she screamed. She began sharing with the church that Peter was free, and no one believed her until they saw it for themselves. I love this reaction as it was a shock for those who were praying and for Peter. It's like a "GOD YOU ARE AWESOME AND YOU HEARD OUR PRAYERS" response. When the victory is won, manifestation has come. It's likely that PRAISE will erupt from your mouth as a sign of gratitude to God.

Prayer Agents are "Snipers"

I was watching the movie "Extraction" on Netflix and there was a scene where the colonel became a sniper and begin shooting from this unseen high place behind trees onto a bridge. He was seeking to target one man who was protecting a young man from being held for ransom. While scoping out the bridge in attempts to find this man (intended target), anyone who was helping him was taken out with one shot. He found the man he was looking for and shot him in the arm one time.

There was a woman who was helping the targeted man and she too had a gun JUST LIKE THE SNIPER. When she noticed the direction in which the shots were fired from, she knew a sniper was present and did not panic. She changed her positioned to a low place on the ground under a vehicle where she could not be identified. In the calmest form she panned the air underneath the vehicle, aiming her weapon in attempts to locate the sniper from the direction where the shots were fired. Skillful and with patience the woman took her time searching until she could hone in on the gunman. When she found him, she focused in on him and took him out with one shot. The sniper did not see it coming.

What was going on here? The woman became just like her opponent. She became a sniper low on the ground against the sniper who was positioned higher up. She realized that she had the same weapon, instrument, gun, artillery as her opponent. She put herself in the same vein as her target and offered the surprise and delight.

There was no time for yelling and panicking. It was time to target and shoot.

The spirit of the Lord provided me with revelation concerning the scene from this movie, and I want to share it with you. In prayer this is a tactic we need to use where we realize what we are targeting and fighting has NOTHING BIGGER, BETTER, OR STRONGER THAN WHAT WE HAVE. They are using a weapon and it can possibly be the exact same weapon as ours. Their position can be the same as ours, which means that we both have the power to aim and to take someone out. The difference is when prayer agents strike, we kill our target, but when our enemies strike, we get hurt, wounded and scared but, we LIVE!

God is fighting for his army to always defeat and win every battle. The Lord knows what battles we are facing and has promised us victory before we begin the fight. The opposing army of enemies have received permissible authority from God to attack us. Meaning that God approved the attack and it is up to Him to decide the detriment of the harm that can be caused. The attack is used for some of us to be saved from things we didn't need in the first place. The attack is used for some of us who will be harmed extensively and may never fully recover from the harm but keeps their life. The attack is used for some of us to completely defeat the enemy without any harm. There are many layers to the fight but in the end no matter what happens, the Lord declared a winning victory.

When you think about the sniper, they are skilled in how they position themselves to attack. A sniper will not be in a place where they can be identified and seen in a visible state. They win based upon where they are in proximity of their target. Once they are positioned, they find a good posture to remain in that will give them direct access to their intended target. The weapon a sniper uses gives them the ability to focus and place the focus on the target that gives them the direct shot that will kill. A sniper doesn't take their time, neither do they speed up, but they are relaxed in studying their intended target. They discover their every move, their surroundings, and wait for the perfect time to make their kill shot.

In prayer, we must understand that we are not fighting a fight in the natural but spiritual. Knowing that everything in this earth, God has done already. The enemy knows that God has done everything already which is his assignment to distract us from what we are getting ready to experience. Therefore, in prayer you must go with the leading of the Lord. He is the best at guiding you on what to pray, when to pray, what position to be in, and what posture is best. If you seek Him, it will cause you not to shoot aimlessly all over the place and missing the intended target. Prayer should never dance around the target but take things out in one shot.

Prayer is not to distract the target from the kill or warn them that a kill is coming. NO! You pull the trigger, shoot your shot, and hit that target! If it lives beyond your shot, it is okay, there will be another time for you to take them out when they least expect it. God has the final say in that. But you did as you were assigned and that was to position, posture, and shoot. *"What you do by Faith, Favor will back you up."*

Isaiah 61:1-2 AMP

The Spirit of the Lord God is upon me,
Because the Lord has anointed and commissioned me
To bring good news to the humble and afflicted;
He has sent me to bind up [the wounds of] the brokenhearted,
To proclaim release [from confinement and condemnation] to the
[physical and spiritual] captives And freedom to prisoners,
To proclaim [a] the favorable year of the Lord,
[b] And the day of vengeance and retribution of our God,
To comfort all who mourn.

Mission: TO BE SEEKERS OF WORKERS

Prayer agents birth out agencies and are always reproducing the work of the ministry for the kingdom of God. If you were to take a company like Allstate Insurance for example. The name of the company is Allstate Insurance, who lends it's name to it's agency owners. Agency owners develop insurance producers (agents in the making) and it continues from there. The agency owners are in different locations across the country operating in business protocols tailored to their location. However, although agency owners have their own location and protocol for their office, Allstate is the company, brand, and image. Therefore, all business practices are subject to the company's standard and name. Prayer agents work for one name, one brand, and one image and that is the kingdom of God. God produced, created, and anointed prayer agents to be filled with the spirit of Him and reproduce in others, which causes expansion in the kingdom.

Scriptures for Prayer Agents to Meditate on:

Matthew 9:36-38 KJV

When He saw the crowds, He was moved with compassion and pity for them, because they were dispirited and distressed, like sheep without a shepherd. Then He said to His disciples, "The harvest is [indeed] plentiful, but the workers are few. So pray to the Lord of the harvest to send out workers into His harvest."

John 9:4-5 AMP

We must work the works of Him who sent Me while it is day; night is coming when no one can work. ⁵ As long as I am in the world, I am the Light of the world [giving guidance through My word and works]."

Isaiah 50:4 KJV

ᵀʰᵉ Lord God hath given me the tongue of the learned, that I should know how to speak a word in season to him that is weary: he wakeneth morning by morning, he wakeneth mine ear to hear as the learned.

The mission of the prayer agency is for us to find workers to train, impart, and develop them to be partakers with Christ. We must empower them to work, inspire them to connect with God and become knowledgeable in spiritual understanding. Prayer agents are always on the watch to find prospects that are teachable, trainable, skillful, and innovative to be a part of the agency. Remember, agents, man sees the outer, but God sees the heart.(*I Samuel 16:7*) Some agents will not look the part, talk the language, or think like the kingdom but they are exactly who God wants to use because their hearts, spirits, and hunger is there. The Lord chose to use you as a prayer conduit so that you can be the testimony of Jesus Christ to others. Never forget that we all are born into sin and shaped in iniquity, and it is only by His grace that we are able to be used by God. Let's be on the lookout for new talent and new vessels to pour our oil upon/into. We possess the oil, not to keep covered, but to pour as the Lord instructs us to. Lastly, I want to close with this scripture

Isaiah 62:6-7-AMP

On your walls, O Jerusalem, I have appointed and stationed watchmen (prophets),
Who will never keep silent day or night;
You who profess the Lord, take no rest for yourselves,
And give Him no rest [from your prayers] until He establishes Jerusalem
And makes her a praise on the earth.

Agents place this scripture on your desk at work, in your vehicles, and inside of your home. The word says we are never silent day or night and we give the Lord NO REST *until.* The word *until* means when we arrive at our destination. We never stop praying, crying, weeping, or travailing until we reach God and God reaches us. The result of all prayers should be PRAISE. If there is not a praise to offer, it could be that you have not reached your *"until"* place just yet. Praise seals up the victory, it is the part where we celebrate.

Prayer agents give attention to the inner man, advance the spiritual man, are educated in the spiritual things of God, and are never overlooked by God but are receptacles and reproducers for the kingdom of God.

Colossians 1:9-13 AMP

For this reason, since the day we heard about it, we have not stopped praying for you, asking [specifically] that you may be filled with the knowledge of His will in all spiritual wisdom [with insight into His purposes], and in understanding [of spiritual things], ¹⁰ so that you will walk in a manner worthy of the Lord [displaying admirable character, moral courage, and personal integrity], to [fully] please Him in all things, bearing fruit in every good work and steadily growing in the knowledge of God [with deeper faith, clearer insight and fervent love for His precepts]; ¹¹ [we pray that you may be] strengthened and invigorated with all power, according to His glorious might, to attain every kind of endurance and patience with joy; ¹² giving thanks to the Father, who has qualified us to share in the inheritance of the saints (God's people) in the Light.

Prayer Agents by Jackie A. Jones Jr.

Prayer

The Authors Covering

Father I pray for every person who has taken the time to read this book in pursuit of seeking something new as it relates to their prayer relationship with You. I touch and agree with them now as what has been read through this book has entered into the gates of their ears and eyes so that they may be open to fresh vision and hearing IN THE NAME OF JESUS. LORD, now move upon the desires of their hearts and allow them to go deeper into Your word, Your presence, and Your will. Speak to Your people in visions and dreams, give interpretations of those vision and dreams right now. Lord, give Your people confidence in prayer. Teach them your ways, oh God, where they can become fluent in prayer, retainers of Your word, receptacles of Your glory, and always growing in the knowledge of God. Father reward them for their faithfulness and bless the works of their hands. Redeem the time wasted on previous seasons of stagnation, lack of knowledge, and procrastination. Father, as spoken in this book, we now align under a new identity and that is for us to be prayer agents. We desire to advance Your kingdom by any means, so that You can get the glory. Lord, teach us how to mentor, develop and expand the work of the ministry by adding those people who are hungry and thirsty for righteous living. God, I speak now to those who are like Jonah and pray against the spirit of fear, worry, doubt, or confusion and ask, Lord, that You will cause them to receive activation like Jeremiah. Stretch Your hands over the lips of Your prayer agents. Put Your words in our mouths so that we shall say what You want us to say. Father strengthen our inner man, our spirit man, and educate us in the spirit of God. Lord, we are ready to do ministry healed, delivered, and right as You guide us through. We give Your name the praise, the honor, and the glory. IN JESUS'S NAME, AMEN!